SEE YOU THURSDAY

See You Thursday

Jean Ure

DELACORTE PRESS/NEW YORK

Published by
Delacorte Press
1 Dag Hammarskjold Plaza
New York, N.Y. 10017

This work was first published in Great Britain by
Kestrel Books.

Manufactured in the United States of America

First U.S.A. printing

Designed by Judith Neuman

Library of Congress Cataloging in Publication Data
Ure, Jean.
See you Thursday.
Summary: Sixteen-year-old Marianne, lonely and
uncomfortable at the expensive girls' school she
attends, finds an unexpected friend in her mother's
new lodger, Abe Shonfeld, a young piano teacher who
has been blind since birth.
[1. Blind—Fiction.   2. Physically handicapped—
Fiction]   I. Title.
PZ7.U64Se   1983   [Fic]   83–5217
ISBN 0–385–29303–8

SEE YOU THURSDAY

1

>>>

ON THE GREEN FELT BULLETIN BOARD IN THE CORNER OF
the classroom, prominently pinned between an appeal for
contributions to the school magazine and a tart reminder that
Camera Club subscriptions were now overdue, was a notice
that read: *Would everyone coming to the Easter party please
write their name below (Sgd) E. Walker, Organizer.*

Around the word "their" was a large red circle and an
exclamation point, and *Well, Betty, I really must say "Hell's
bells!" (Sgd) F. Jones, English teacher.* Underneath that was
a long list of names, starting with Mary-Jane Mountain, who
was always the first to sign up for anything, and ending with
Emily Rivers-Smith, who was never quite sure. Marianne,
surreptitiously casting her eye down the list while rather too
obviously studying the mimeographed copy of the fire regulations, had no need of counting to show her what she already
knew: every name was there except hers. Five from the
junior class, ten from the sophomore. Everyone who was entitled to go was going, except her.

"Have you signed up yet?"

Beth Walker. (Organizer.) Always so bustling—always so
busy. Marianne, with a creditable start, tore herself away
from the fire regulations and carelessly said, "What?"

"I said, have you signed up yet? Easter party? Are you coming?"

"Oh—" She shrugged a shoulder. Uninterested. Above it all. "Probably. Haven't decided."

"Well, I wish you'd make your mind up. I need to know the numbers, I've got to get things started."

Why? thought Marianne. What was all the rush? It was months away yet. They were still only at the beginning of February. Come Easter—

"You're the only one who hasn't," said Beth. She said it accusingly. "You don't have to fork out the two quid immediately, you know. It's only the numbers I want."

"I'll think about it," said Marianne.

As if she had been doing anything but. She had been thinking about it for the past eighteen months. Since even before that—even back in the freshman year it had been a weight on her mind. She had seen it there, looming ahead of her. Desperately she had tried to argue that she ought not to bother going into senior high—she ought to be out earning her living, start making some sort of contribution to the household budget. Alas, neither her mother nor Miss Warrender would have any of what they chose to call "that sort of nonsense." Her mother had said, quite crossly, that she hadn't pinched and scraped and slaved all these years only to have Marianne throw it back in her face by walking out of school at the age of sixteen and ending up behind the counter in Woolworth's. (Woolworth's, for some reason, had always been her special bugbear. It was never "behind the counter in Littlewood's," "behind the counter in the British Home Stores." Always Woolworth's.) Miss Warrender, playing the wise headmistress, had said gently but sternly that she mustn't be frightened by the prospect of hard work. It would all be worth it in the long run, and "I'm sure you can do it if you really try."

How could you explain that it wasn't the work that you were frightened of? That what was poisoning the whole of your existence and making your life wretched beyond endurance was this miserable, loathsome party? You couldn't. It was too humiliating. They would think you were some sort of social inadequate. Sometimes she thought so herself.

She had lived the last few months praying that a miracle would happen, but of course it hadn't. The school hadn't burned down, the party hadn't been cancelled (there had once, a couple of years back, been talk of it, when a local resident had complained of cuddling going on in the rosebushes), Marianne herself had not been stricken with any dire disease nor run over by a passing truck. The most she could hope for now was to fall down the stairs and break a leg.

Miss Jones, who was also their class teacher, arrived for double English period. *Paradise Lost.* Satan and his beastly fall. Of Man's First Disobedience, and the Fruit/Of that Forbidden Tree, etc., etc., etc.

Who but Milton could have an opening sentence twenty-six lines long? Despite herself, her attention wandered. The bulletin board was directly in front of her. From where she sat she could see Beth's notice quite clearly. *You're the only one who hasn't signed up.* . . . She felt her palms grow sticky. If Beth had noticed it, it wouldn't be long before everyone else did too.

"There are only fifteen names down here. Who's not coming? Oh! Her! Well, of course, she never does. I mean"—scornful laugh—"who could she bring? I've never seen her anywhere with anyone."

No, because she didn't know anyone to go anywhere with. She bent her head, cheeks blazing. Unthinkable—unthinkable!—to turn up without an escort. Never in the whole history of senior high parties—it was the whole point and purpose of parties. You had to have *some*one. A cousin would do, or even a brother; but *some*one. To arrive by oneself—the sweat trickled wetly down the center of her chest. Familiar waves of panic washed over her. Suppose she tried to brazen it out? Said she had better things to do? Said her boyfriend was away in Africa? India? China? Signed her name and then had a brain hemorrhage at the last moment?

It wasn't any use. They would never believe her. They would all know it was a lie. *I've* never seen her out with anyone—

" 'That to the height of this great Argument/I may assert Eternal Providence/And justify the ways of God to men.' Right. Marianne! Should you care to expound?"

Expound? Expound what? What did she mean, expound?

Doom-laden, Marianne rose to her feet. O God, she thought, before the end of term let an aircraft crash on us. . . .

It was Miss Jones who crashed on her, and long before the end of term. As the four o'clock bell rang, she gravely told Marianne to stay behind. Without preliminaries, as the door closed behind Emily Rivers-Smith and they were left alone, she said, "You know, Marianne, that you're not going to get through your exams at this rate?"

She wasn't going to get through them anyway. French and English, she was supposed to be taking. It might just as well have been math and physics for all the chance she stood, except that at Combe House you couldn't study math and physics at advanced level. Only arts subjects. If you wanted to study science you had to transfer, which was the reason why the entire senior grade consisted of no more than sixteen persons and why just one of those persons not attending the Easter ghastly party would be as instantly noticeable as Ludgate Hill without St. Paul's, as Nelson's Column without Nelson at the top of it, as—

"You seem distracted," said Miss Jones.

Her voice had become kinder. Her attitude had softened. Any minute now she was going to invite confidences. Her face, already, was composing itself into lines of ready sympathy and willingness to enter into problems. Marianne squirmed in anticipation.

"There's nothing wrong, is there? Nothing troubling you?"

She denied it as a matter of course. It was strange with Miss Jones. She tried so hard and meant so well; why could she never learn? One would sooner pour a can of gasoline over one's head and set fire to oneself than expose one's innermost doubts and fears to a person one had to see every single day of one's school existence. What self-respect could one have, knowing all the time that she knew?

Miss Jones, as always, remained oblivious. "I've been noticing just lately . . . these last two semesters. You're not the girl you used to be. I realize you're at a difficult stage just now"—Marianne looked at her warily—"but it's this antisocial trend that bothers me. You don't seem to participate—you don't join in and do things."

Her chin went up. "I came to Open Day."

"Only because you had to. In any case, that was the whole school. I'm talking more about class events. Why is it, I wonder, that I never seem to see your name down for anything?"

Marianne mumbled, "My mother . . ."

It wasn't really fair to blame her mother. It was true she did get into a bit of a flap over things, like going off to her bridge evenings and leaving Marianne in the house to be raped and murdered—"Whatever you do, *don't take the chain off the door*"—but not as much of a flap as all that. She wouldn't have raised any objections if Marianne had wanted to go on the trip to Brighton or to the theater. She would have issued countless instructions about not missing the last train home and not accepting lifts from strangers, as if she were still a simple-minded ten-year-old, but to do her justice she wouldn't have made any fuss about being deserted. With all her faults, you couldn't call her possessive.

Miss Jones, with quick understanding, said, "Of course, I was forgetting . . . she's on her own, isn't she? Your fa—"

"He died," said Marianne. She always told people that he had died. It saved explanation, and anyway he might just as well have done, for all that she had ever seen of him. It wasn't so very much of a lie.

Miss Jones was nodding sagely. "And there are just the two of you? Yes. That is always an awkward situation. I daresay you're very close to each other?"

Marianne grunted noncommittally. She would not have said that they were—but again, she would not have said that they weren't. If that was what Miss Jones wanted to think—

"Believe me," Miss Jones said earnestly, "I do know . . . I know exactly what it's like. But for your own good—would it help, I wonder, if I were to come around and speak to her?"

The horror was such that she could only stand there, dumb.

"You see, for her sake," said Miss Jones, "as well as for yours . . . you do have your own life to lead. I'm not asking you to be selfish, but sometimes it *can* be kinder to be just a little bit cruel. Certainly it's no kindness to let her become too dependent on you."

Guilt galvanized her, at last, into speech.

"She's not dependent," said Marianne. "She's got a job."

She worked for a firm of attorneys, Kingsley, Montague & Simons. She had been there for the last five years, ever since she had insisted on sending Marianne to Combe House instead of the local public high school. She worked part-time as a clerk for Mr. Simons, ten o'clock to four, four days a week. She wasn't dependent on Marianne in any way at all.

"Of course I wasn't speaking financially," said Miss Jones. "One can be just as dependent emotionally."

"If you mean that she *clings*—" said Marianne.

She had got herself into this mess, trying to put the blame on her mother; not that some of it wasn't her fault. If she hadn't been so stubbornly set on "a good education," meaning How Now Brown Cow, and the Duchess of Somewhere for Speech Day, and special red twill shoe bags with one's initials hand-embroidered, Marianne could have gone to the public high school along with everyone else and none of this dreadful business would ever have arisen. They had boys at the public school. She would have known dozens and dozens of them.

Miss Jones, in thoughtful fashion, was stacking books.

"I don't expect," she said, "that it's a question of her clinging, so much as you conceiving it your duty to stay at her side."

Marianne blinked. It was amazing—truly amazing—how someone who called herself a qualified member of the teaching staff could get things so grotesquely wrong. Still, she wasn't going to put her right; not again. These attempts at intimacy were really quite awful. Really hot-making. How could she go *on* like that? Now she was saying about "week-

ends doubtless being very precious—I know they were for me."
Now she was fantasizing about "just the two of you together"
and "not liking to leave her by herself."

"But at your age—at your time of life—you really should
be mixing . . . you really should be getting out."

"I do get out," said Marianne. "I get out quite often."

"But not with other people. You keep yourself aloof. What
clubs do you belong to? What group things do you do?"

She muttered: "I don't go for group things."

"It worries me, you see. You shouldn't be so isolated.
What friends do you have out of school? Do you have a
boyfriend?"

Her cheeks fired up. What right had she? What *right*, just
because she was in a position of authority, to go poking
around in other people's private lives? How would she like
to be asked if she had a boyfriend? Especially when she
almost certainly hadn't. You hardly could, at that age. Miss
Jones, not waiting for an answer, becoming brisk once again
as she sensed defiance, said, "You're not a child any more.
You're sixteen, it's time to start making an effort. There are
some things we all find difficult, but that's part of growing up.
Coming to terms with ourselves. Forcing ourselves to stand
back and take a long, clear look. How are you going to cope
with work if you don't like doing things with people?"

"I don't mind *doing* things," said Marianne.

It wasn't doing things that bothered her—she was perfectly
happy to be in the basketball team or the nativity play, or
whatever else they wanted her to take part in—it was *not*
doing things that presented all the difficulties. Just being in a
big aimless group doing nothing. That was what she wasn't
good at.

"Well," said Miss Jones, "let us hope to see an improvement. I notice you haven't yet signed up for the Easter party? I take it you will be coming?"

The way she said it, she made it sound almost like a threat.

"It would look rather conspicuous, don't you think," said Miss Jones, "if you didn't?" She paused a second. "Have you given any serious thought, by the way, to what you're going to do when you leave school?"

She had, but it hadn't really got her anywhere. She had toyed, in a vague and unspecified sort of way, with the idea of social work—at any rate, something to do with people. Wild horses now would not have dragged the admission from her. Something to do with people? And she accused of isolationism? She could imagine the pitying smile.

"It's time you bent your mind to it," said Miss Jones. "You've got a brain, if you'll only use it, but you're not going to be an easy girl to fit in."

Marianne tossed her head, with its long, honey-colored plume of hair, at present pulled back into an elastic band in accordance with school rules.

"I'm not that bothered," she said. "I don't go so much on this work ethic thing. I'd just as soon opt out and be a breeding machine."

For a moment there was silence. She wondered if she had gone too far. Miss Jones considered her awhile, lips pursed, then she turned deliberately and picked up her books.

"I wouldn't advise it just yet, Marianne," she said. Her voice was light and dismissive. "For a girl of sixteen, you are still quite extraordinarily immature."

2

‚‚

THE JOURNEY HOME BY BUS ACROSS THE BUSY CENTER OF
town took her a good forty minutes. Miss Jones's remark
rankled every inch of the way. *You are still quite extraordinarily immature . . .* what made it rankle all the more was
that she had a nagging suspicion herself that it might be true.

The bus reached Old Town and she fought her way off,
through shopping bags and strollers, into the usual wedge of
bodies that thronged the narrow pavements. Some of Old
Town had been built in Elizabethan times. Now, mostly, it
was dilapidated Victorian terraces and garish modern shop
fronts: typical south suburban. Marianne was the only girl in
either of the senior grades to live out this way. Most of the
others came from the smart areas over on the other side, the
fashionable side, with the big detached houses and neatly laid-
out private estates. It was one of the reasons why she almost
never saw any of them out of school. Not that she was
ashamed of living in Old Town, in an end-of-terrace with a
garden that backed on to the railroad—she would rather live
there any day of the week than in a plastic box with garden
gnomes—but somehow she didn't seem to have all that much
in common with them. In any case, it took forever, trudging
into the center of town and then out again. One ought to
make friends with people who lived close.

Tip had lived close, just around the corner over the baker's shop, but Tip and her family had gone off to New Zealand almost a year ago and since then Marianne had found it increasingly difficult to make friends with anyone at all. It was difficult, of course, to replace somebody who had been special. She and Tip had been known as "the twins." They had done everything together, had no secrets, kept nothing back. Tip wrote now from New Zealand to say that she had met this fabulous boy who was called Jo. He sheared sheep and his eyes were blue and he had the most fantastic suntan and "Honest, I kid you not, I am quite excruciatingly *gone*." Whatever turns you on, Marianne thought sourly. She wouldn't want a sheep shearer herself. When she wrote back, she purposely didn't mention Jo. She knew it was mean—she knew, deep down, that it was only jealousy. The trouble was that knowing it didn't make it any better. It still didn't take the ache away.

She turned up Star Street, pulling off her school hat as she always did on the home stretch. She couldn't very well remove her blazer and her sweater and her tie, but she could at least get rid of the hat. Old Mrs. Derwent, in slippers and apron, was out on the pavement at number nine watering her window box. Marianne, rather shyly, said good evening. She was never quite sure how Mrs. Derwent felt about her. Once upon a time, years and years ago, she and Stephen Derwent, who was Mrs. Derwent's grandson, had been in the same class at elementary school. Sometimes, out of school, when he had come to visit the old lady, they had actually played together. They had ridden their bicycles and chalked hopscotch squares on the pavement and played marbles in one or other of their back gardens. Then, of a sudden, it had all gone sour. She still remembered the day that it had happened. She had been peacocking about the street in her new green blazer ready for Combe House next semester and Stephen had stopped dead at the sight of her and stared and said: "Yer not going *there*?"

"Yes, I am," she had said, and she had felt hurt and angry because he was making it sound as if it were her fault—as if *she* had any choice in the matter. "What's wrong with going there?"

Stephen had screwed up his face and said, "Snob school, innit? 'Swhere they send yer when yer can't get nowhere else."

This had been so disastrously near the truth (her mother had dreamed of Rosemount, but you had to be really rich to go there; really rich or really clever, one or the other) that Marianne had flared up instantly in her own defense.

"Well, at any rate, it's better than where *you're* going . . . *any*one can go to *Hill*side. You don't even have to *pay* to go *there*."

She and Stephen hadn't talked from that day to this. They had crossed paths once in a local movie theater, and both had been embarrassed. She often thought, if she had gone to the local high school, Stephen Derwent might by now have been her boyfriend instead of her sworn enemy.

She arrived indoors to find her mother preparing baked beans.

"Not *again*?" she said. "Not two nights *running*?"

From under the broiler came the smell of burning toast. Mrs. Fenton, who wasn't one of the world's great chefs even at the best of times, snatched defensively at the broiler pan.

"It's all there was—I didn't have time to get to the shops. We had an urgent completion out at Bromley, I've only just got back. In any case, you've already had a hot school meal."

"School meal!" Soggy French fries and two lumps of gristle.

And now *baked beans*. It was obviously one of those days. She let her briefcase fall to the floor with a loud thud. Mrs. Fenton, affecting not to notice, said, "Set the table, would you? And choose what fruit you want to follow. . . . I think there are some cherries somewhere."

She found the cherries hidden away behind the canned fruit salad and sliced peaches. They were, she knew, intended as a sop—as a peace offering to make up for baked beans. Usually when she said "cherries" she was curtly told: "Money doesn't grow on trees, you know." Pushing her luck as she jabbed in the can opener, she said, "Don't suppose there's any cream?"

"You can take the top of the milk, if you like."

Top of the milk? She eyed her mother suspiciously. Stealing cream from the top of the milk was one of those crimes that ranged along with putting hot mugs on polished tables and using too much dishwashing detergent. To be offered both cherries *and* top of the milk struck her suddenly as a trifle dubious. What was she going to be asked to do? Saturday morning shopping by herself? Take the sheets to the launderette? Sunday tea with the Simonses? Please, God, anything but *that*.

Rather overcasually, putting out the baked beans on pieces of scraped toast, Mrs. Fenton said: "Got much homework to do tonight?"

She was tempted to say, "Yes! Heaps and heaps!" but curiosity got the better of her. She said guardedly: "Not an awful lot; why?"

"I'd like you to give me a hand with the front bedroom, if you would."

"*What?*"

"I said, I'd like you to give me a hand with the front bedroom. . . . It shouldn't take too long, it only needs a vacuuming and a bit of a dust and polish and check the dishes are clean and—"

Her mother's eyes met hers across the table. The message in them was quite clear: we don't want any scenes, do we? She knew she ought not to make one. She knew she ought to control herself. At least she didn't explode all at once. Dangerously, she laid down her knife and fork.

"We are not," she said in a small, tight voice, "having *another?*"

"Look, I know you don't like it, and neither do I, but the way things are—"

"*Christ!*"

"Marianne—"

"I thought we'd *finished* with all that? After Miss Pargeter, you said—you *said*—"

"I know what I said, but the fact is we need the money."

"We wouldn't need the money—we wouldn't need *half* the money—if you didn't insist on throwing it away on useless school fees when I could be being educated for free!"

Mrs. Fenton gestured, impatiently. "We've had this out before. There's no point in going into it all over again. It's a matter of principle. So long as I *can* pay for your education, I *will*. It's one of those sacrifices that I choose to make."

"Yes, and one that we all have to pay for! Baked beans and no vacations and"—she choked—"*lodgers!*" She had truly thought, when Miss Pargeter departed for a better world, that they had seen the end of that particular form of torture. Having lodgers was just about the worst degradation that could be inflicted. *Don't do this, you'll upset the lodger. . . . Don't do that, the lodger won't like it.* Think of the lodger. Always the lodger.

"It won't be as bad as it has been." Mrs. Fenton spoke soothingly, placatingly, as if to a hysterical child. "I daresay we shan't see all that much of him. He'll be away most weekends, and—"

"*He?*" Momentarily diverted, she forgot about her anger. "You're not having a *man* in the house?"

Could she be hoping to have an affair with him? It was exactly the sort of thing one read about. Women were always hopping into bed with their male lodgers. It wasn't beyond the bounds of possibility. Her mother wasn't as old as all that, and now she was actually blushing, which almost seemed to confirm it.

"Of course," she said, "I wouldn't normally. It was only that Mr. Simons asked me, as a special favor, whether we'd be prepared—seeing as he's a friend of the family—"

"Who is?"

"Mr. Simons. They're clients of his—well, it's the Lawrences, actually, who are the clients, but—"

"So who's coming here?"

"Mr. Shonfeld."

"Who's Mr. Shonfeld?"

"He teaches music—up at Rosemount."

Rosemount. I bet if it had been Hillside, thought Marianne, she wouldn't have been so keen to have him. Not even for her precious Mr. Simons.

"Why's he want to come *here?*" she said.

"Principally because he needs somewhere within easy reach. He's been commuting from Victoria every day, but it's got a bit too much for him, so—" Her mother pushed her plate away, knife and fork laid neatly side by side. "The fact is—you might as well know straight away, and I don't want any stupid reaction—he happens to be blind. That means you're going to have to be a great deal tidier around the house than you are now. No more cluttering up the hall with hockey sticks and tennis racquets, they'll all have to go away in their proper places—and no more leaving things lying about in the middle of the floor, either. At least it will be good from that point of view. And that reminds me . . . you can put a tack in that bit of carpet on the stairs at last. You were supposed to do it weeks ago. Heaven knows, it's only a five-minute job. You can do it tonight, while I'm checking the dishes. We don't want him breaking his neck before he's even had a chance to find his way about. Now what's the matter? Why have you gone all quiet?"

"I haven't gone all quiet."

"Yes, you have. Are you sulking?"

She pursed her lips. "Why can't he go into a hostel, or something?"

"Well! That's a very charitable attitude, I must say."

"Miss Pargeter was bad enough—*she* was only *senile*."

"Marianne, I really am surprised at you. I thought you were the one who was always so keen on social justice and helping those who couldn't help themselves."

She sniffed. There was a world of difference between helping people voluntarily and having them thrust upon you. "I hope he doesn't think we're going to *wait* on him?"

"Of course he doesn't! Don't be so stupid and intolerant. He's perfectly accustomed to doing things for himself. He may need a bit of a hand now and again, but I presume even *you* wouldn't grudge taking him round the supermarket once a week?"

She scowled. "How's he going to cook?"

"I don't expect he will, very much. He'll have a hot meal midday, and I—I said he'd be quite welcome to come down and join us for breakfast in the mornings. It won't make an atom of difference to you, you're only ever there long enough to cram your food into your mouth and go rushing off, so—"

"A *stranger* at *breakfast?*" Marianne jerked her chair back across the kitchen floor. "That is just about the *end.*"

It was all she needed. The day was almost perfect in its misery. She was immature, she was an isolationist, and now there was to be a stranger every morning for breakfast.

"You can put the cream back on the top of that milk," she said. "*I* don't want it."

3

>>>

ON SATURDAY MORNING A PIANO ARRIVED. IT WAS ONLY A
very small piano, but still the men who brought it had to
remove the window frame from the front bedroom window
and hoist it up with block and tackle, and still they managed
to scrape the paint while they were about it. Mrs. Fenton was
all graciousness. She said it really didn't matter, the house
was due for repainting anyway.

When the window frame had been put back and the men
had had cups of tea in the kitchen and departed, Marianne
crept upstairs and stood looking at the piano. Her fingers
itched to touch it. She tried the lid, but of course it was
locked; she had to be content with just looking. She had had a
piano of her own once, an aged upright with two of the keys
missing. It had been an inheritance from her maternal grand-
mother, the only thing in all her life that she had ever in-
herited, and in spite of not being able to afford lessons she
had still managed to teach herself to sight-read and pick out
hymn tunes with one finger. Given time she might even have
graduated to proper music—she could already do the opening
bars of the Golliwog's Cake-walk—but alas! the piano had
been found to be harboring woodworm and that had been the
end of it. Her mother had said that in any case it had disturbed
the lodger. She supposed it didn't matter now if the lodger

disturbed her. She went back downstairs to put the question and see what the answer was: the answer, very briefly, was "Don't be so silly."

"Why am I being silly? How can I be expected to do homework with someone crashing about on a piano on the other side of the wall?"

"You can do your homework downstairs."

"I'll still hear it."

"No, you won't. He's not going to play concertos."

"Well, what about when I'm in bed? He won't need to play concertos, just scales'll be enough."

"He's not going to play it when you're in bed. We've already come to an arrangement. He's given me his word . . . he won't touch it before seven in the morning or after ten at night. Goodness knows, you're never in bed before that—I do wish you would remove all that rubbish from the hall. This is the third time I've asked."

Grumbling, she began to collect up the usual conglomerate of hockey stick, hockey boots, muddy boots, mildewed parka, walking shoes, sneakers. "Where's it all supposed to go? Where am I supposed to put it? Talk about *fuss*."

"You want to be responsible for someone breaking his neck? Just try having a bit more consideration. How would you like to be blind? Take it upstairs and make room in the closet. It shouldn't be in the hall in the first place. Anyone would think we were running a second-hand clothes shop."

Marianne, scooping up armfuls, said: *"Honestly."*

The lodger was due to arrive "some time after lunch" on Sunday. As soon as the last plate had been dried, the last spoon put away, Marianne snatched up her parka (hanging now from a hook on the kitchen wall) and made for the back door.

"I'm going for a ride."

"Just as you like. You'll only get soaked—it's going to pour before the day's out."

"Bit of rain doesn't bother me."

A bit of rain was nothing compared to having to stay in and see the lodger: breakfast time tomorrow would be quite bad enough. She took her bicycle, old and clanking but still serviceable, from the shed, wheeled it down the garden, out through the narrow passage that ran the length of the terrace, separating backyards from railroad. Half an hour of hard pedaling and she was out in the country, in greenbelt land, where the grass grew free, unencumbered by concrete, and the air smelled sweet from nettles and cow.

She parked her bicycle where she always parked it, by the little old church with its neat, mossy churchyard; set off on foot up the lane by the side of the cottages, past the field where earlier in the year there had been winter lambs, past the second field, shaped like a triangle, where sometimes there were horses that would come and take handfuls of plucked grass, or maybe an apple if she thought to bring one, on up the rutted cart track with its piles of fresh cow; turn left through the woods, stiff climb to the top, squelching through the winter slush, dodging the trailing branches; then out once again into the open, looking down into the patchwork valley, skirting the disused chalk quarry with its high fence up which the bindweed coiled and twined; across the buttercup field and into her Kingdom.

She had discovered the Kingdom almost a year ago—just about the time when Tip had gone off to New Zealand. Once it had been a farm. Now it was abandoned, the buildings in ruins, windows shattered, roof beams charred, old farm implements left out in the open to rust and to rot. One little corner of it she had appropriated for her own. Behind a low, tumbledown barn, whose walls were sagging and sides wide open to the elements, was tucked a small building scarcely any larger than a good-size garden shed. It had presumably been used for storing things—grain, to judge by the fine dust that still covered the floor—but its roof was intact, its walls still solid, and since nobody else had seemed to want it, she had claimed it for herself.

Bit by bit, over the months, she had made it habitable. Her first piece of furniture had been a couch—a child's mattress, to be strictly accurate. Exploring the surrounding area one day, she had stumbled across it in a dump, where vandals had come stealthily by car in the dead of night to dispose of the rubbish they no longer wanted. There had been builders' rubble and car parts, the burned-out wreckage of a television set, a couple of pieces of machinery—and the mattress. She had known at once that she must have it. Determinedly she had lugged it all the way back, dragging it behind her over the rough ground. She had left it out in the open for a whole week (fortunately it had been summer) just to make sure, but nothing had crawled out of it and it had smelled quite clean. Since then, from the same dump, she had rescued an old car seat upholstered in leather, a kitchen chair without any back, and an oval rug, which had once had a pattern and even now had some wear left in it. From home, at various times, she had smuggled an old cushion, a moth-eaten army blanket, cutlery, dishes, a vase for flowers. With her pocket money she had bought a plastic bucket, which she left out in the yard to catch rainwater, and a plastic bowl for washing up in. She kept her Kingdom tidier by far than she ever did her bedroom at home, not just because it was hers, but because she felt responsible for it. She liked to think of it when she wasn't there, and she liked to think of it as happy and cheerful and clean.

In summer when the weather was warm, she went to the Kingdom every weekend with a knapsack full of food and books and useful odds and ends—can opener, pictures for the wall, tablecloth for the chair that had no back. There she would quite often spend the entire day, walking, dreaming, reading, whatever took her fancy, enjoying the luxury for once of being in command. It was her very own bed-sitting room, where she might be by herself and get away from lodgers. No one to tell her what to do and when to do it; no one to dictate. If she wanted to lie on her back with her hands behind her head and stare up at the ceiling doing nothing, then that was what she would do, and for just as long as it pleased her to do it.

Today, before she had been there even half an hour, the heavens opened and the rains came down. The roof had sprung a leak and she had to set her plastic washing-up bowl under it to catch the drips. The door kept rattling in the wind, there were drafts she had never noticed before. Suddenly it was lonely and cold, not at all the place for daydreaming: home exercised its pull, in spite of the lodger. At the first break in the downpour, she pulled up the hood of her parka and set off down the mud-swirled path to the woods.

She arrived back in Star Street with her hair looking like seaweed, to find her mother talking to a strange girl in the kitchen.

"Oh, Marianne," said Mrs. Fenton. "There you are. I told you you'd get wet. This is Sarah—Sarah Lawrence. Mr. Shonfeld's niece. She's been helping Mr. Shonfeld settle in."

Marianne said, "Oh." Sarah Lawrence turned her head to

look at her. She was younger than Marianne. Probably no
more than fourteen—say fifteen, if she was a midget. It didn't
stop her giving herself airs. There was something in her dark-
eyed gaze that seemed to Marianne to betoken impatience:
Who is this utterly unimportant creature who has interrupted
us? They studied each other very briefly. Marianne's gaze was
hostile, Sarah Lawrence's disdainful. She could afford to be
disdainful. From her top to her toe—from curly, cropped
head to tiny, suède-booted feet—everything about her was
perfection. Marianne, conscious of her own bedraggled state,
hair streaming and feet slopping about in muddied Hush
Puppies, felt long and lanky and uncouth. She resented it,
in her own kitchen. She nodded rather curtly. Sarah Lawrence dipped her neat head in acknowledgment, then briskly
turned back to Mrs. Fenton, addressing her with an air of
authority as one adult to another.

"I've shown him where everything is. Mostly it seems to be
all right. I've told him, if he needs anything, to come down
and ask you."

Oh, had she? thought Marianne. She pulled off her dripping parka and shook it. Sarah Lawrence stepped back a
pace.

"There's only one problem, and that's the stove. I'm afraid
he's not used to gas."

"Not used to gas—" Marianne mimicked the words in her
head. She took up the towel and began toweling at her hair.
Silly self-important cow.

Her mother, giving her a look, said: "I'm sure he'll soon
get the hang of it. He's only got to shout if he finds himself in
difficulties. Now, what can I offer you? A cup of tea? Cup of
coffee?"

"It's very kind of you, but I'm afraid we really haven't the time. We're meeting Mummy and Daddy up in town. We've got tickets for a concert."

"Oh. Well, if you're quite sure—"

"Very sure. Thank you all the same." She turned, self-possessed, to the door. "There was just one thing—"

"What was that?"

"About tomorrow. I know the bus stop is just up the road, and of course I'll show it to him when we leave, but—"

"Oh, you needn't worry about tomorrow." Cheerfully, Mrs. Fenton removed the sodden parka from the draining-board and hung it over the clothesline. "No problem there—Marianne uses the same stop. She can easily take him in with her in the mornings."

Marianne, standing with her head muffled up in the towel, wondered for a moment if she had heard correctly. *Her?* Escort some blind man in and out every day? Why should she have to be encumbered with him? She wasn't the one who wanted to curry favor with Mr. Simons. Slowly, unbelievingly, she emerged from the towel. Sarah Lawrence was looking at her. Considering her, no doubt; summing her up. Was this great ungainly girl really to be trusted with the care of her precious uncle? Marianne stared back at her haughtily. As if aware of antagonism, Sarah tilted her chin and said: "You'll only need to show him once. He's quite used to getting about by himself."

Marianne stuffed the towel back over the rack. She thrust her damp hair behind her ears. "Doesn't make any difference to me."

"Might even ensure punctuality," said her mother. "Now where are you off to?"

"Going to wipe my bike down."

"You might at least stay and say hallo to Mr. Shonfeld."

"I can say hallo to him tomorrow, can't I? They're in a hurry now. Got to go to a concert." She wrenched open the door and paused, with the rain coming in. "I do hope you have a good evening," she said.

Marianne was in bed when the lodger arrived back, by himself, from his concert. She heard the front door open and close, heard him slowly making his way up the stairs. First step, second step—she hadn't put that tack in. She hadn't put that *blasted* tack in. *That's the third time I've asked—* God, don't let him trip over it! There would be hell to pay. *How many more times? Never do a* THING *that I ask you—*

Third step. Fourth step. Breathe again. First thing tomorrow morning—yes, I *will*! I swear it! She would make an effort and she would wake up early. She would go downstairs and she would do it before anyone was about. She would bang her head on the pillow, six times, very hard, and—

The lodger had reached the top. He seemed to have stopped, she couldn't hear footsteps any more. She stiffened, straining both ears. What was he doing? Had he lost his bearings? Forgotten which way to turn? Cold wet goose bumps tingled up her spine. If he were to come barging into the wrong room—

The lodger moved on, across the passage; *tap tap tap* with his stick like Blind Pew. The sound was eerie in the darkened house. Marianne shivered, pulling the bedclothes farther up about her shoulders. There was something unnerving in the thought of a blind man being out there, just on the other side of the door, creeping about in the blackness.

She lay on her back, listening. His door had opened, he was in his own room. No click of the light switch, that wouldn't be any use to him. Instead, a series of small, un-identifiable noises, as of someone feeling his way round an unfamiliar place. She pictured him, like a mole, groping and fumbling. She knew she ought to be charitable, and so in theory she was, but this wasn't theory, this was cold, hard, horrible fact: the lodger had come and was creeping about in the room next door, and tomorrow, God help her, she was to take him in on the bus.

She wondered glumly what he would look like. He would be old, of course; she took that for granted. Anyone who was a friend of Mr. Simons had to be old. Old and hunched, with dark glasses for his eyes and crumply black suits that smelled of mothballs.

From the room next door came a loud thud, followed by the unmistakable smash of broken glass. Marianne heaved over onto her side, buried her head beneath the pillow. She had said all along that he would keep her awake. Much good it was going to do putting a ban on piano playing if he in-tended to spend half the night breaking things.

Grimly, she crammed the pillow down hard over her ears. This semester, she thought, was turning out even worse than she had anticipated.

4

SHE HAD GENUINELY INTENDED TO GET UP EARLY AND DO THE carpet. Unfortunately, although she woke in time, she could not immediately remember what it was she had woken for, and before she had a chance to clear her brain and think about it she had fallen back to sleep again. The next thing she knew, her mother was hammering at the door and shouting: "Marianne! It's half past!" the way she always did. Then she remembered: the lodger had come and she hadn't tacked down the carpet.

She pressed her ear to the wall and could hear the lodger on the other side. He was moving about, doing things. She pictured him getting dressed, in his crumply black suit and a stiff collar and tie. At least he hadn't yet fallen down the stairs and broken his neck. That was something to be thankful for.

She threw back the covers, tore with the speed of greased lightning into her clothes, galloped full tilt across the bedroom, and bolted out through the door.

Slap bang, straight into the lodger.

She recoiled, horror-stricken. "I'm f-frightfully sorry—"

The lodger, just managing not to fall headfirst down the staircase, said equably: "That's all right. My fault . . . ought to look where I'm going."

Marianne turned scarlet, even though he couldn't see her. She was appalled to discover that he was quite young. At any rate, not old. Certainly not thirty—maybe not even twenty-five. She felt tricked. How could *he* be anyone's uncle? Uncles were at the very least middle-aged. Not that she had ever had any of her own, but—

The lodger, with a smile, said: "You must be Marianne. We didn't meet yesterday, did we? You were out doing things with your bicycle."

"Yes—I mean, no—"

He wasn't even wearing a crumply dark suit and a collar and tie. He wasn't wearing a suit at all. He had on a perfectly ordinary pair of cord Levi's and a yellow sweater that she wouldn't have minded for herself. Nervously she took the hand that he was holding out.

"I hope you enjoyed your c-concert," she said.

"Yes, I did. Very much. I only hope I didn't disturb you when I came in?"

She swallowed. "N-no. Not at all."

"I had a bit of an altercation with the corner of the table." His smile broadened into a grin—apologetic, but still a grin. As if it were something amusing, to have an altercation with the corner of a table. "I'm afraid I broke a glass. I'll replace it, of course."

Cavalierly, taking it upon herself, she said, "You don't have to bother. I break them all the time."

"Ah, yes," he said, "but it's your house."

At least he appreciated the fact—it was more than that stuck-up niece of his had done. She still didn't understand how he could be her uncle. He looked more like her brother. He had the same dark, cropped, curly hair and square jaw, and really a most enviable sort of profile, just so long as he kept it as a profile and didn't spoil it by turning toward you. The effect was ruined when he did that, because then it became obvious that he couldn't see, and there was still something creepy about it, even in full daylight. So long as he remained in profile he looked perfectly ordinary and no different from anyone else. Even, almost, quite attractive. She thought her mother might have had the goodness to warn her. It was disconcerting, to say the very least, when you had been bracing yourself for another geriatric like Miss Pargeter, to find yourself suddenly confronted instead with a man not even old enough to be your father. It threw the whole thing into a totally different perspective.

Mr. Shonfeld, apparently not disconcerted in the slightest, said pleasantly, "Am I going in the right direction? Turn left at the foot of the stairs?"

She said, "Yes, that's right"; and then, remembering, added, "You have to be careful on the next-to-last step, the carpet's up."

Mr. Shonfeld said that he would watch out for it. Marianne stood a moment, wondering what one did. Did one go rudely dashing down the stairs in front of him, three at a time, in one's usual fashion, or did one politely stand back and wait for him to go first? Mr. Shonfeld solved the problem for her by waving her ahead and telling her to carry on.

"Don't bother waiting for me, you'll be all day . . . I tend to be a bit tortoiselike until I get used to places."

Guiltily, because gladly, she plunged forward. "I'll go and get a hammer and put a tack in the carpet."

Last night, she had been worried only as to what her mother would say. She hadn't really cared two straws about the lodger breaking his neck. It was difficult to care very much about someone you hadn't seen, especially when you had already dismissed that someone as old and hunched and doddery. Now that she had actually set eyes on him and discovered him not to be any of those things, she knew that if he were to break his neck all because of her, she would be haunted by it for the rest of her life.

She burst into the kitchen and snatched open the middle drawer of the chest, where they kept the one hammer and the one screwdriver and the tin of assorted nails. Her mother, prodding things in the frying pan, said, "If you're going to tack the carpet at last, don't bother. I did it."

"Oh." She shut the drawer, abashed. "I'm sorry, I forgot."

"So what's new?"

"I said I'm sorry."

"Yes, well, it wouldn't have been very nice, would it? There's the kettle. Can you get it?"

As she made the tea, Marianne said, "Is he really her uncle?"

Mrs. Fenton looked amused. "Why? What were you expecting? An octogenarian? You haven't forgotten, I hope, that you're taking him in on the bus."

"No," said Marianne.

That was something she had not forgotten. Taking Mr. Shonfeld in on the bus had temporarily ousted even the Easter party from the forefront of her worries. She didn't know what she was expected to do. Must she take him by the arm? Lead him by the hand? Or must she just walk at his side and make sure he didn't bump into things? Did she talk while she was doing it, or did she keep silent not to distract him? And once they had actually managed to get aboard the wretched bus, how was he going to know where to sit? Was it up to her to show him, or did he find out for himself? It was all very well, calmly saying that Marianne would take him in on the bus, but nobody told her *how*. She wouldn't want to embarrass him, doing things that didn't need to be done. It had been bad enough when she had thought he was going to be old and doddery; it was even worse now that he wasn't.

Mr. Shonfeld appeared at the kitchen door and brightly said good morning, and was he on time. Mrs. Fenton said, "Absolutely. On the dot. Marianne, show Mr. Shonfeld where to sit."

She was doing it again. *Show him where to sit.* How?

She stuck the tea cozy on the teapot, scraped back a chair, and said, "Would you like to sit here?"

Mr. Shonfeld closed the door behind him. He took a couple of paces, rather uncertainly, into the room and then stopped. Mrs. Fenton was gesturing urgently. She seemed to be making some kind of gathering motion. Awkwardly, Marianne plucked at the sleeve of Mr. Shonfeld's sweater.

"Over here," she said.

He moved forward obediently. Mrs. Fenton nodded, in a way that said, *That's better.* Marianne pulled a face. How was she expected to know? Some blind people didn't like you doing things for them.

For breakfast there were frankfurters and tomatoes. Mrs. Fenton announced the fact with a brisk: "Here we are, then . . . frankfurters at twelve o'clock, tomatoes at six." Marianne wondered what on earth she was talking about, until slowly it dawned on her that she was describing for Mr. Shonfeld's benefit the position of things on his plate. Grudgingly she admitted it to be the sort of simple, practical assistance that she herself would never think of offering—but *why frankfurters?* They never had frankfurters; not for breakfast. Frankfurters were supper. She couldn't eat them at quarter to eight in the morning. Darkly she looked at Mr. Shonfeld

across the table. Don't say he was going to turn out to be
some kind of religious freak who didn't eat bacon. Mr.
Simons didn't eat bacon. For crying out *loud*.

She tried to work up a feeling of indignation, but it
wouldn't come. It was like trying to get mad at someone
when they were asleep. Mr. Shonfeld sat there not knowing,
eating his breakfast without being able to see it, and even if
he were the cause of loathsome frankfurters, it seemed a bit
mean and petty to hold it against him. She watched him
awhile covertly, from under her lashes, just in case. The fact
that he had a white stick and crashed into the corners of
tables didn't necessarily mean that he couldn't see anything at
all. She wouldn't want to be caught staring at him, though
from the way he felt around for his teacup, very careful not
to knock things over, she thought perhaps there wasn't much
danger of it. How awful for him if he really couldn't see
anything—if he didn't even know when it was nighttime or
when the sun was up. He raised his head and for a moment he
seemed to be looking at her, and quickly she turned away, but
when she looked back again his eyes were gazing straight past
her, over her shoulder, at nothing. It made her feel quite
odd.

Her mother, catching her attention, frowned at her and
jerked her head toward her untouched breakfast. To spare
Mr. Shonfeld's feelings, she forced herself to eat it. Her
mother would only say: "What's the matter with those frankfurters?" if she didn't, and then she would have to say that
she didn't feel like frankfurters and then Mr. Shonfeld might
start thinking about bacon and eggs and wondering if it were
his fault. She still wished to goodness that he wasn't there, but
since he was, she wouldn't want to hurt him.

At quarter past eight, they set off up Star Street. Marianne carried her briefcase, fat with school books and a clean shirt for gym, with her hockey stick held lengthways and hockey boots tied on to the handle. Mr. Shonfeld had a satchel, presumably containing music (but what use was music, if he couldn't see to read it?), which he carried slung diagonally across his chest the way first graders did. It seemed rather lowering, for a grown man, but she supposed he needed to keep a hand free. The satchel had his initials stamped on it in gold: *A. F. S.* She wondered what the *A* stood for. Adam? Anthony? Alexander? She didn't like to ask him—she didn't like to say anything to him at all, in case it was the wrong thing to do. As the garden gate had closed behind them, Mr. Shonfeld had said: "May I?" and placed his hand on her arm. Now, stiff with embarrassment, she held her arm like a ramrod and didn't dare to move it by as much as an inch lest he think she was uncomfortable, which actually she was, because her arm was starting to ache quite atrociously from being so rigid. If he had only turned out to be old and hunched she could have coped with the situation. It was his being young that made it so embarrassing. People didn't expect young men to be led about by schoolgirls.

The journey to the bus stop, which usually took about fifteen seconds flat, because usually she was late and had to run, seemed this morning to take more like fifteen minutes. She knew she couldn't ask Mr. Shonfeld to run, but she was sure it would be far easier if she were to take him by the arm and guide him. They would certainly get along far faster. She only hesitated because perhaps he might not like it. Perhaps it made him feel safer, going along at his own pace. How could she know? She didn't know anything about blind people. She had never had anything to do with them. It wasn't fair, expecting her to look after him. Why couldn't he get a guide dog?

They reached the bus stop at last. Timidly, she shepherded Mr. Shonfeld across the pavement.

"This is where we have to wait. . . . There are about five hundred people here. There always are."

Mr. Shonfeld smiled and said, "I see." It seemed a strange expression to use, in view of the fact that he couldn't, but he smiled quite nicely even if it wasn't exactly focused anywhere. "What number bus do we wait for?"

"I have to get a ten. You could get anything, but the ten's the only one that goes my way."

"Then I'd better wait and get one with you. . . . Don't want to take any chances the very first day!"

She wondered, for just a panic-stricken second, whether she was expected to get on whatever bus came and get off when he did and actually see him as far as Rosemount. Her mother hadn't said anything about doing that. She'd only said, "Take him in on the bus." Nothing about getting off and getting on again. Tentatively, she said, "Do you—know your way? At the other end?"

"Yes, indeed! I've been having practice runs for the past two weeks . . . know it like the back of my hand! Could almost get there blindfolded."

She wasn't sure whether she was supposed to laugh at that or not. Mr. Shonfeld, obviously sensing uncertainty, laughed for her.

"Honestly! I know it down to the last lamp post. I've even counted the cracks in the pavement . . . couldn't get lost if I tried! All I need is to be shoved out at the right spot and pointed in the right direction and I'll be fine."

She was relieved to hear it. The idea of having to escort him all the way up the hill to Rosemount had made her go quite hot and cold.

A number ten had appeared. It was beached like a stranded whale on the edge of a sea of traffic, but already the line was starting to shuffle and bunch in anticipation.

"The bus is here," said Marianne.

Nervously she took hold of Mr. Shonfeld's arm. He didn't seem to mind, but obediently moved forward with the rest of the line. What with getting them both safely inside and not losing contact in the crush, she almost forgot about feeling embarrassed. As for finding seats, there wasn't any question: they had to stand, squashed together, by the door.

"Is it always like this?" asked Mr. Shonfeld.

"Yes. Like a cattle truck, but you're only on for a few stops."

He nodded. "I'll be able to find my own way tomorrow. You won't have to nursemaid me."

She hoped he wasn't saying it because of anything that she had said or done. "I don't mind," she said.

"No, but I must learn to be independent. That's the whole object of the exercise."

Was it? She hadn't known. She had thought it was just the journey in by train being too much for him.

"What about tonight?" she said.

"Oh, I'll be all right tonight. You don't have to worry about that. I'll get someone to put me on the bus."

"But how will you know where to get off?"

"I've got a tongue in my head!"

Of course he had. He wasn't an idiot. All the same—

"It's not so easy, coming back," she said. "You have to cross over. Twice. And it's ghastly at that hour."

"Well, I shall just have to risk it, shan't I? I daresay if I stand still for long enough some kind person will take pity on me. They do; you'd be surprised . . . the number of times I've found myself whisked across to the other side of the road without even wanting to go there!"

Marianne hesitated. After fiddling with the strap of her briefcase for a bit, she said, "If you like—if you don't mind hanging on for ten minutes—I could always walk up and collect you." As soon as she'd said it, she turned bright pink. Collect him! As if he were a child. "I mean," she mumbled, "if you're leaving at the same time as I am—"

"Four o'clock?"

"Yes. But it would take me ten minutes—"

"So long as you're quite sure it's not going to put you out. I don't want to make a nuisance of myself. It must be quite bad enough for you as it is, having me cluttering the place up, banging into tables at eleven o'clock at night."

Bright pink turned to scarlet. "That's all right," said Marianne.

"You mustn't think I'm always going to be asking you to do things for me. I have to learn how to manage."

Yes, she thought; but he couldn't manage two major crossings at quarter to five in the afternoon. Not on his very first day.

"This is your stop," she said. Without giving herself time to wonder whether it was the right thing to do, she put a hand under his elbow. "I'll see you at four. . . . I will be there, I promise."

5

>>

AT SCHOOL, BEFORE PRAYERS, MARY-JANE MOUNTAIN looked at the notice on the bulletin board and said, "I suppose you're not coming?" She might have added, *of course*, but there was no need. It was there in her tone.

Marianne, stung, said, "Who said I'm not coming?"

"You haven't signed up."

"For heaven's sake! Is that all? Give me a pen and I'll sign up now! Anything to keep you happy."

Mary-Jane watched skeptically as she scrawled her name. Marianne knew exactly the thought that was going through her head: I'll believe it when I see it. . . .

"Who are you going to bring?"

"Who are you?" she said, though she knew perfectly well who Mary-Jane was going to bring because Mary-Jane had a boyfriend called Barry who was going to be a second Laurence Olivier and was at the Royal Academy of Dramatic Art even now learning how to set about it. Every girl in the school could have recited the whole of his life history by heart. It had been Barry this and Barry that for the past two terms.

Mary-Jane said nothing but only smiled in a silly, secretive, condescending sort of way. Another girl, peering short-sightedly at the addition of Marianne's name to the list, said, in a voice of unconcealed amazement, "Oh, are you *coming?* Who are you going to bring?"

"Someone," said Marianne.

Mary-Jane and the newcomer exchanged knowing glances. "Who's someone?" Mary-Jane asked.

"Someone I know."

"Who?"

"Where does he live?"

"What does he do?"

"What's his name?"

Faced with a barrage of questions, Marianne began to flounder. "What's it to you?"

"Interested, that's all."

"Don't you want to tell us?"

"Why not?"

"Go on! Don't be bashful . . . what's his name?"

Recklessly, she said, "Adam." It was the first name that came to mind. Not that it mattered. It probably wasn't really Mr. Shonfeld's name, and anyway he would never know.

"Adam what?" said Mary-Jane.

"What does he do?"

"Is he a student?"

"He's not a *cousin?*"

"Haven't got a cousin."

"So what is he?"

"What's he do?"

"I bet he's still in school!"

"He isn't still in school." Who wanted a boyfriend who was still in school? Still running around in a blazer, subject to authority? She might just as well do the job properly while she was about it. "He left school eons ago."

"So what does he do?"

"He's—he's a musician," said Marianne.

Their eyes widened gratifyingly. "*Really* a musician?"

"Yes," said Marianne. "Really a musician."

"What's he into?"

"What's he play?"

"Is he with a group?"

She toyed for one heady moment with the honor and glory of making him a lead guitarist or somebody's drummer but had just sense enough at the last second to reject it. There would only be more questions, and then she would be sunk. She didn't know too much about the rock scene. Mrs. Fenton discouraged it. She said it led to drugs and unwanted babies.

"He plays the piano," she said. "He's into classical."

At least it ought to shut them up.

It did. Only Emily Rivers-Smith, who had pretensions, was impressed by classical.

"Oh!" she said. "A *concert* pianist?"

That was going too far. That was entering the realms of fantasy.

"Don't be stupid," said Marianne. "Where would I be likely to meet a concert pianist?"

She had forgotten, when she promised Mr. Shonfeld to meet him at four o'clock, that Monday evenings they were supposed to stay late and listen to talks by former students on the subject of careers. So far they had had a secretary, a computer programmer, and something called a stock controller. All of them monumentally boring. This evening it was the Civil Service, which looked to be even more monumentally boring.

Quaking slightly, because the talks were Miss Jones's brainchild and Miss Jones was pretty keen on them, plus she was already in her bad books after last week's unfortunate episode, Marianne approached her and explained about Mr. Shonfeld. One thing she was determined about: she wasn't going to let him down. Certainly not for the Civil Service. She had given him her word, and it was impossible she should not keep it. That remark of his about cluttering the house up had shaken her. He undoubtedly *was* cluttering the house up, but the last thing she had intended was to make him feel bad about it. It could hardly be said to be his fault that he was blind and walked into tables.

Miss Jones, though predictably not pleased ("It's a pity you have to miss this particular one. The Civil Service could have suited you very well") nevertheless appeared to appreciate the necessity of someone being there to give Mr. Shonfeld a hand on his first day.

"I take it that by *next* Monday he will have orientated himself? I shouldn't like you to miss two in a row."

"Oh, he'll be all right *next* Monday," said Marianne. "It's only today."

The rest of her class was struck almost speechless. How had *she* managed to get out of it? Marianne said loftily that she had a prior engagement.

"Oh yes?"

"Doing what?"

"Going to meet your boyfriend, I suppose?"

"That's right," said Marianne.

She left them to hum and buzz among themselves and set off up the road at a canter to meet Mr. Shonfeld and take him

safely home. She had told him ten minutes and already Miss
Jones had kept her talking for a good five.

She arrived, panting, at the bottom of Rosemount Hill as
the town hall clock was striking the quarter hour. She could
see Mr. Shonfeld waiting for her, outside the large wrought-
iron gates of the school. He was talking to a girl wearing a
blue and silver tie and a blue blazer covered all over in pins
and badges, which Marianne knew meant senior year. She
was typically Rosemount, poised and willowy, like a society
debutante. Marianne felt a twinge of what might almost have
been jealousy, except that that was absurd. What was there to
be jealous of? *She* didn't want to be poised and willowy like a
society debutante. She didn't approve of society debutantes.

She wasn't jealous of what the girl looked like. She suddenly realized it: she was jealous because she was standing
there talking to Mr. Shonfeld. That was even more absurd. If
she were going to start getting possessive about a lodger
whom she hadn't even wanted in the first place, *and* still
didn't—

The girl turned away and began walking down the hill
toward her. She had lint-fair hair and a face that was perfectly oval, with a serious, rather responsible, expression and
a complexion of purest ivory. Now that she was nearer she
looked less like a debutante and more like a Madonna. Marianne wondered who she was. One of Mr. Shonfeld's pupils,
she supposed. She derived some small and stupid comfort
from the fact that at any rate Mr. Shonfeld wasn't to know
that she looked like a Madonna, any more than he was to
know that Marianne at this moment had a spot on her chin
and that her mouth was too wide and her teeth too big and
her nose the wrong shape and her legs like walking bean-
poles. It was a pity, though, that he couldn't see that she had

washed her hair last night. Her hair was her one real claim to
beauty.

He might not have been able to see her hair, but he had
quite obviously heard her footsteps, crashing and walloping
in her stout school shoes, for already he was turning toward
her with an air of expectancy. Marianne said: "Hallo! I'm
here."

"Hallo," said Mr. Shonfeld. "You sound out of breath."

"Yes. I've been running."

She was about to explain that the reason she'd been running was that she'd left five minutes later than usual, on account of having to stay and speak to Miss Jones, but then she
thought that perhaps he might start imagining she'd only
offered to come and meet him in order to wriggle out of the
careers talk, so she said instead: "It took me longer than I
thought. I was afraid you might be getting worried in case I
wasn't going to turn up."

"I wasn't worried," said Mr. Shonfeld. "I knew you would
if you said you would."

Taking Mr. Shonfeld back wasn't nearly as bad as bringing
him in had been. For one thing, she knew now what to expect. It didn't pulverize her with embarrassment when he put
his hand on her arm, even though they were surrounded on
all sides by hordes of homegoing Rosemounters, who stared.
She only tossed her head and thought, Let them stare—stupid
gaping sheep. Mr. Shonfeld might be their music master, but
he wasn't living in their houses. *She* was the one who was
responsible for him.

When they got off the bus at the other end Mr. Shonfeld
asked her if she had the time to "do me just one more favor. . . .
Your mother said there's a supermarket on the corner. Could
you possibly bear to take me around there?"

The prospect, last week, of having to drag a blind man around a supermarket had appalled her; now she quite liked the idea. It filled her with a pleasing sense of her own usefulness, her own good citizenship. Besides, Mr. Shonfeld was already ceasing to be "a blind man" and becoming simply Mr. Shonfeld, who happened not to be able to see.

She managed the expedition rather efficiently, she thought. She took a shopping cart, so that she could dump her briefcase in it, and starting at the beginning, with the dairy produce:—"Butter? Bacon?" (He didn't *say* that he didn't eat bacon, but on the other hand he didn't express any interest in buying any.) "Cheese? Eggs?"—she led him right to the exit without missing so much as a single section, nor having to go back once upon her tracks. The place was seething, as usual, with last-minute shoppers grabbing what they could on their way home from work, but she found she had only to say: "Excuse me" in a loud enough voice for a path, miraculously, to be cleared. Aggressive women with shopping baskets, who would normally have elbowed her to one side, took one look at Mr. Shonfeld and couldn't flatten themselves fast enough. It made, thought Marianne, a pleasant change.

Mr. Shonfeld, not realizing, said: "Well! That was all very easy." She didn't like to tell him that it wasn't usually so. She had read somewhere, once, in some magazine article, that people with disabilities hated to be treated in any way differently from people without. He might feel humiliated, perhaps, if he thought that allowances had been made.

Frowning as she removed her briefcase from the cart, ready for checkout, Marianne said, "You haven't bought very much." He had stuck rigidly to foods that could be eaten cold. She had tried to tempt him with chops—lamb, not pork, just in case—but he had only smiled and shaken his head. "I hope it's not going to be *dinner*," she said.

Mr. Shonfeld laughed. "Not all in one night, certainly!"

"*Any* night—" Baked beans on toast was miserable enough; but sardines, and cold tongue, and *yogurts*! "It's winter," she said. "You need something hot."

Mr. Shonfeld, defensively, said: "I already had a hot meal at school."

"School!" From what she'd heard, Rosemount's hot meals were no better than anyone else's, despite the place being so posh. "If it's the cooking that bothers you," she said, "I don't mind helping."

"No!" His voice was very firm. "I must learn how to manage on my own."

"But if you're not even going to try—"

"I will. In time . . . just as soon as I've stopped being terrified of burning the place down!"

Monday being Mrs. Fenton's free day, she had produced a beef casserole. Marianne, as she ate it, kept thinking of Mr. Shonfeld upstairs opening a can of sardines.

"Why don't we give him evening meals as well?" she said.

"What?"

"Evening meals as well as breakfast."

"What are you talking about?"

"Mr. Shonfeld . . . he's eating sardines."

"Oh! Well, maybe he likes sardines."

"He doesn't. He's scared of using the gas."

"He'll soon get accustomed to it. In any case, he can always come and ask."

"He doesn't want to come and ask, he wants to be independent. . . . We could at least give him something on Mondays."

"Then he wouldn't be independent, would he?"

"He would the rest of the week."

Mrs. Fenton said: "Start as you mean to go on. He's already getting a cooked breakfast."

And a hot school lunch, thought Marianne. Whatever we do, we mustn't forget the school lunch. She speared a chunk of meat, large and succulent, such as had never been seen in any school lunch since school lunches began.

"He's scared he'll burn the house down."

"I don't imagine there's much likelihood of it."

"No, but you can see, if he's not used to it—" She closed her eyes and tried imagining, just for a moment, how it must be to be Mr. Shonfeld. "Why don't we get a hotplate?"

"Because there's no separate meter up there for electricity."

"We could always get one put in."

"Not without a lot of expense. Anyway, what makes you so concerned? This time last week you'd have thought I wanted to billet an entire army on us, the way you were carrying on. Now, it seems, you'd like to see me running some kind of deluxe hotel."

"I didn't say anything about a deluxe hotel. I just said why not get him a hotplate."

"And I said because it would mean installing a second meter. . . . What's with the sudden change of heart? Do I take it the idea of a new lodger isn't quite as paralyzingly ghastly as you thought it was going to be?"

"It's every bit as ghastly and I loathe it." She scowled. "That doesn't mean I can't feel sorry for him . . . sitting up there by himself eating sardines. . . . How am I expected to enjoy *this*"—she gestured at her plate—"knowing *that*? There is such a thing as common humanity."

"Funny," murmured Mrs. Fenton. "There didn't seem to be, a week ago . . ."

6

‡‡

NOT FOR WORLDS WOULD SHE HAVE ADMITTED IT TO HER
mother—pride, for a long while, prevented her admitting it
even to herself—but, truth to tell, having another lodger in
the house was *not* the pain she had thought it was going to be.
Mr. Shonfeld really could not have been said to be any
bother. It was surprising how quickly you could grow accustomed to the sight of a strange face at the breakfast table, and
it was only Mondays to Fridays when all was said and done.

On Friday evenings he went straight from school to his
married sister (who was Sarah Lawrence's mother and lived
up in town). He rarely arrived back until quite late on Sundays. Thursdays, too, he was usually out, which really only
left Mondays, Tuesdays and Wednesdays, and even then he
was so quiet you hardly knew he was there. Mostly he stayed
in his room and played the piano, but not anything loud,
nothing strident or clashing. It seemed most often—from
what Marianne could make out with an ear pressed to the
wall—to be Haydn and Mozart and that sort of stuff. Sometimes he had the radio on, but only ever a murmur. Miss
Pargeter and her television set had gone full blast halfway
through the night. After ten o'clock, in strict obedience to his
agreement, Mr. Shonfeld didn't play anything at all.

Often, as she lay in bed listening to the silence, Marianne

felt that it wasn't quite fair. He ought at least to be allowed his radio. She, after all, could lie in bed with a book, but what could Mr. Shonfeld do? He did have books of a sort; she'd seen them in his room, great unwieldy-looking tomes—Braille, she supposed they were—but for the life of her she couldn't imagine how anyone ever succeeded in reading from them. She was perfectly certain that she would never have the patience to master all those fiddling little combinations of dots. Mr. Shonfeld, when she had ventured one morning on the way up to the bus stop to ask him about it, had only smiled and said that she would do it quickly enough if she had to. "It's all a question of motivation. . . . If it's a choice between reading slowly and not being able to read at all . . ."

Not being able to read at all was a prospect almost too horrific to contemplate. It was that which made her lie in bed at ten o'clock at night and listen to Mr. Shonfeld doing nothing and feel that it really wasn't fair. He ought at least to be allowed his radio.

She tried broaching the subject with her mother. "It wouldn't disturb *me*. *I* wouldn't mind. I can sleep through anything."

"You couldn't sleep through Miss Pargeter's television set."

"That was different. That was television."

"You mean, that was different, that was Miss Pargeter. . . . You just stop troubling your head about Mr. Shonfeld. He didn't come here to be cosseted, he came here to find his feet and learn how to manage. If he wants help, he'll ask for it."

"He doesn't want help, he just wants to play his radio."

"How do you know? Have you asked him?"

"No, but—"

"Well, then, there you are. . . . The same rule applies to everyone. I don't expect *you* to play your radio after ten P.M., I don't expect him to play his."

"But it isn't fair! He can't—"

"Marianne." Her mother, very firmly, put an end to the conversation. It was a thing she had an annoying habit of doing. "Leave Mr. Shonfeld to fight his own battles. He's perfectly capable of it. He doesn't need you to do it for him."

It was true: Mr. Shonfeld didn't need her to do it for him. Her fears that he would expect to be waited on had proved quite groundless. Miss Pargeter had been ten times the amount of trouble that Mr. Shonfeld was. With Miss Pargeter it had been a never-ending stream of "Marianne, I wonder if you would mind—if you would be so good—if you could possibly—" She seemed to have spent half her life running errands for Miss Pargeter. Mr. Shonfeld almost never asked her to do anything. Perhaps if a letter came he might ask her to read it for him, and once he had asked her if she could look up a number in the telephone directory, but there was never any question of taking advantage. She never had to "just pop up the road" for him three times a week, or "just empty his trash basket" every other day as she had for Miss Pargeter. She still went with him to the bus stop every morning, but only because they left at the same time and it would have been churlish not to, not because he needed it—not because he asked it of her. Sometimes, too, in the evenings, if they were both going straight home, she would walk up to Rosemount to meet him, because two major crossings at the other end still weren't easy for him, but even that he could cope with if he had to. He didn't actually depend on her. He really didn't depend on anyone for anything. As Sarah Lawrence had said, he was quite used to getting about by himself.

When he came in late at night now, he no longer stood hesitating at the top of the stairs, or had altercations with the corners of tables. When it came to breaking glasses, Marianne broke far more than Mr. Shonfeld.

One of the very few areas where he genuinely couldn't manage on his own was shopping. He needed someone to tell him what was on the shelves and what the prices were. It had become Marianne's regular weekly task: every Tuesday evening after school she would take him to the supermarket. Even then he worried that he was inconveniencing her.

"It isn't inconvenient," she said. On the contrary, she quite looked forward to it. She liked to feel herself in charge, making suggestions, advising him what to buy. "You ought to have fresh fruit. Bananas, or oranges, or something . . . apples are good. What about apples? What about a can of soup? What about *eggs*? Eggs are nutritious. You ought to have eggs. Have half a dozen eggs and a can of soup."

Even eggs and soup, she reasoned, were better than endless cups of yogurt and cold sardines. If he only opened a can and put the contents in a saucepan, it would be an advance; if all he did with the eggs was boil them, it would at least force him into making acquaintance with the gas stove.

One week she said, "You ought to have meat. Why don't you try lamb chops? Anyone can cook lamb chops. All you've got to do is stick them under the broiler and do a few potatoes—buy a package of peas—there's nothing to it. After all, you've got to start some time. You can't exist on eggs and soup forever."

Mr. Shonfeld, smiling slightly, said, "No, miss."

"Well, you can't. It's ridiculous. Men *do* cook nowadays. It isn't clever any more to be useless."

She thought when she'd said it that she ought not to have,

though she'd only meant that thank heavens the old lines of demarcation had gone, that men these days did women's things and women did men's, and that if she could put a plug on the electric heater then Mr. Shonfeld ought to be able to cook himself a lamb chop. She hadn't meant anything personal, but still, perhaps, it had not been very tactful. In fact, it had not been tactful at all. Covered in confusion, she swung away. Lamb chops, of a sudden, had become offensive. She wished she had never suggested them. Why should he not eat his eggs and his soup if that was what was easiest for him? What right had she to interfere? She was becoming a carbon copy of Miss Jones, what with her preaching and her—

"Marianne!"

She froze, abruptly. Now she had gone off without him. As if it wasn't bad enough, telling him he was useless, she had now gone off and left him standing there. That was the last time he would let *her* take him to the supermarket. Her face shone like a crimson sunset. She turned back, dragging the cart behind her.

"I'm sorry, I—"

"Oh, don't apologize! I've no doubt I deserved it. You're quite right—I've got to start some time. Look, take me back, and buy me a lamb chop, and I promise"—he held out a hand—"that I will do my best to render it fit for consumption."

"I could always come up and show you," said Marianne. It seemed the least she could do, considering it was she who had pushed him into it. "I've only got to show you once, and then you'll be able to do it for yourself."

This time, after a moment of hesitation, he accepted her offer. "But only if you're quite sure your mother won't mind."

"Oh, *she* won't mind," said Marianne. In any case, it was her bridge night: she wouldn't be there to mind. Not that there could be any possible objection, but at least it would save having to explain. One didn't want to be accused of cosseting.

She enjoyed showing Mr. Shonfeld how to cook lamb chops. She had never particularly liked cooking before, but teaching someone else added a whole new dimension. Mr. Shonfeld kept apologizing for being stupid and clumsy, but she was used to being pretty clumsy herself. Her mother was forever complaining that she had only to walk into a room at one end for vases to go crashing floorward at the other. She felt nothing but sympathy, therefore, when Mr. Shonfeld knocked over the salt, and could perfectly understand it when he sent the frozen peas scattering halfway across the carpet.

"Just don't worry," she said, down on her hands and knees gathering them up. "It's not important."

Some of his plates and cutlery hadn't been washed up too well. She didn't like to mention it, because she knew it must be difficult for him, but when she tried surreptitiously to do it in the basin without his noticing he guessed at once what she was up to.

"What's the matter?" he said. "Have I left things filthy?"

"Not filthy," said Marianne.

"Just disgusting. . . . Now you see why I don't cook."

"Yes, but you must eat. After all"—she scraped at some egg that was stuck on the back of a spoon—"I don't expect the ancient Britons ever bothered washing up at all."

She wasn't too sure, the following Tuesday, whether Mr. Shonfeld would want to go to the supermarket with her again, considering the way she had bullied him the previous week, not to mention walking off and abandoning him. She thought perhaps he would make an excuse—that he didn't need anything, or one of the girls from school had already taken him—but on the way home, he said cheerfully, "What are you going to make me cook this week? Spaghetti?"

She looked at him rather shyly, not sure whether he was serious or teasing.

"Do you really want to?"

"Of course I really want to! Would I ask you if I didn't?"

He might, she thought. He might, just to show willingness. On the other hand, he *ought* to know how to fend for himself.

"Only trouble is," she said, "I'm not sure that I can do spaghetti."

"Well, it doesn't have to be spaghetti. I'm not your actual spaghetti freak. It was just something that sounded easy."

"How about scrambled eggs? They'd be easy."

"Okay, so let's make it scrambled eggs. I should think even I might be able to manage that—but only on one condition: you stay and eat it with me. I'm not going to sit there gorging myself again when it's you that's done all the hard work."

She didn't mind about the hard work, and anyway it was far harder for him than it was for her, since she was only there in a supervisory capacity, but she had not the least objection to staying and having a meal with him. It did seem rather silly, Mr. Shonfeld up there on his own and her down in the kitchen finishing Monday's leftovers. If she was going to teach him how to cook, she might just as well stay and share the results with him. Her mother could hardly complain that she was intruding (Mrs. Fenton was very hot about not intruding: "Guests are guests; they're entitled to their privacy") when it was Mr. Shonfeld himself who'd invited her.

"All right," she said. "We'll have scrambled eggs on toast and I'll bring up the rest of yesterday's pie, or she'll wonder why I haven't eaten it."

All things considered, Mr. Shonfeld didn't do too badly. Admittedly he knocked the salt over again—though that could have been said to be her fault, for not warning him it was there—but he only really broke one egg over the side of the bowl, and not all of it dripped onto the floor. Marianne, mopping it up, said, "I'll show you omelettes next week, if you like"—and then instantly grew flustered, because he hadn't actually asked her to show him anything next week, had he? Mr. Shonfeld, however, only said, "I wish you could show me how to be less ham-fisted."

"It just takes practice," said Marianne.

"Sure. Like playing the piano—except that playing the piano strikes me as being a sight easier than cracking eggs into a bowl. Has that one gone in?"

She looked up from her mopping operations. "Most of it."

"That means two thirds of it hasn't. Don't humor me."

"Well, don't bash them so hard. You're not breaking dinosaurs' eggs."

"If I don't bash them, they don't break at all. They've got shells like rubber—they just bounce." He reached out for another one. "What about you, Marianne? Do you play anything? Piano, recorder—"

Under the table, Marianne scrubbed viciously. "No," she said. "She chopped it up."

"She did what?" Mr. Shonfeld sounded surprised. "Damn! It would help if the bowl would keep still. Chopped what up?"

"My piano."

"Chopped it *up*?"

"It had woodworm—at least, that's what she said. She took it out in the garden and chopped it up and made a bonfire of it."

"Sounds a bit extreme."

"It was probably *illegal*—it wasn't even *hers*. *And* I could almost play the Golliwog's Cake-walk." She stood up, critically surveying the progress of the egg cracking. "Try holding the bowl with one hand and the egg with the other. You'll find it ever so much easier."

"Ah. Yes. I see—it is, isn't it? That's much better. Did you ever have lessons?"

"No, but I could at least pick things out with one finger. I'll bring you a bigger bowl next week. That one's ridiculous."

"It's all right. I'm managing. You know, you're always welcome to come in here and pick things out with one finger. I could even give you a few lessons if you like. Would you like? In return for showing me how to crack eggs? I wouldn't feel so bad then about letting you do things for me."

She gaped at him, mouth ajar. "Do you mean it?"

"Why not? If you've got the time, Tuesday evenings—then there's weekends. I've no objections if you want to come in and tinker about when I'm not here. Entirely up to you. There! That's the last one. Now what do we do?"

By the time they had successfully cracked and scrambled half a dozen eggs and placed them on pieces of toast and were sitting down to consume them, Marianne felt bold enough to put a question she had been longing to put ever since that very first morning when she had taken Mr. Shonfeld in on the bus: "What do the initials *AJ* stand for?"

There was a slight pause, then Mr. Shonfeld said: "The *J* stands for Jonathan."

"What about the *A*?"

"I almost blush to tell you what the *A* stands for. I always think my parents must have had some kind of brainstorm. The *A* stands for Abraham."

"*Abraham?*"

"Yes, I know! Don't tell me!"

Politely she said, "One can't help what one's called. Mine had to go and pick on Marianne."

"I don't see anything wrong with Marianne."

"It's affected, that's what's wrong with it. I wouldn't have minded plain Marian—but Mari*anne*."

"Imagine if it had been Polyanthus, or Marigold . . . how do you suppose *I* feel, saddled with Abraham?"

It was certainly an awe-inspiring thought. She was glad she hadn't known about it before.

"I'd thought that it might be Adam," she said.

"Would that it had been!"

"Is it what people actually call you? *Abraham?*"

"Not if I can help it. Mostly they shorten it to Abe."

She was relieved. Abraham was awful. Abe was quite catchy. "Is it all right if I call you Abe?"

"Well, I certainly shan't respond to Abraham!"

"No, I mean . . . I don't have to go on calling you Mr. Shonfeld?"

"It would seem a bit futile, wouldn't it? Now that you've forced me into revealing the ghastly truth."

"Whatever do you suppose"—she looked at him earnestly across the table—"made them do it?"

"God knows! Abraham Lincoln? Excess of Jewish patriotism? Your guess is as good as mine. . . . Why do parents do half the things they do?"

Yes, thought Marianne; why did they? Most of them were quite senseless. Getting married only to get divorced, having children and never seeing them, making sacrifices that nobody wanted . . .

"Did you really and *honestly* mean about the piano lessons?" she said.

"Of course I really and honestly meant about them."

"Now?"

"If you're ready. All you have to do is take a seat—"

Things could have been worse. They could have been a great deal worse. Having another lodger really wasn't turning out too badly after all.

7

>>>

Mrs. Fenton was horrified when she heard about the free lessons; she said that it was imposing.

"It isn't imposing," said Marianne. "He offered."

"I don't care. I won't have you accepting charity."

"It's not charity!" She was indignant. "It's fair exchange—I'm teaching him how to cook."

Mrs. Fenton, pursing her lips, said that that was different.

"How is it different?"

"It's not your living, for one thing. Just remember that he's been doing it all day long."

"Abe doesn't mind. It was his suggestion. He *likes* teaching people to play the piano—he thinks it's a great pity more people don't. *He* thinks it's a pity I wasn't taught before."

Mrs. Fenton looked at her sharply. "Did Mr. Shonfeld give you permission to call him by his Christian name?"

"It's not a Christian name."

"Don't quibble! I said, did he give you permission?"

"*Yes!* I asked him! I asked him what his initials stood for, and he said Abraham Jonathan and that I could call him Abe, and it's not a Christian name, it's Jewish, and heaven only knows why we're not eating bacon because he isn't in the *least* bit religious, he doesn't care two straws, he—"

"I hope," said Mrs. Fenton, "that you haven't been pestering him with impertinent questions."

"Impertinent!" She tossed her head impatiently. What was impertinent about it? Abe didn't mind her asking—he didn't mind her asking him anything. He was one of the easiest people she'd ever met. You could talk to him about whatever you liked. You didn't have to stop and think, you just said whatever came into your head, he never took offense. He hadn't been the slightest bit offended when she'd asked him about bacon.

"Would it sink me irretrievably," he had said, "if I said what about it?"

"You mean it doesn't bother you?"

"Doesn't bother me what I eat. Ought it to?"

"Well!" Indignation had known no bounds. There they had been, stuck with lousy frankfurters, interspersed with the occasional boiled egg, and all for no reason. Abe had been quite apologetic.

"Sorry if I've shattered an illusion. Did you think I was going to come complete with prayer shawl and sidelocks?"

"Well . . . no," she had said. "Not *exactly* . . ."

"But you think I ought at least to lay off the bacon?" He had pulled a face. "I'm obviously not living up to expectations. I'm afraid I'm not really what you call a terribly good sort of Jew. I do go to the synagogue occasionally—like about once or twice a year—"

She had hastened to reassure him. "I only go to church about once a year, too—then only when I have to. Carol service, and such. I'm not really a terribly good Christian. In fact"—it had come upon her, quite suddenly: a revelation—"I'm not a Christian at all. I'm not anything."

Upon reflection, Abe had said he rather thought that he was not anything either. "Just me."

It had seemed to Marianne to be a bond between them. Now her mother was saying it was impertinence. How could it be impertinence? After an intimate conversation like that? It only went to show how very little she understood. She plainly had not the least idea what Abe was like. To her he was still "Mr. Shonfeld"—still the lodger.

"If you don't let him give me piano lessons," said Marianne, "he won't let me teach him how to cook. Do you really want to be responsible for him having to go on eating nothing but yogurts and sardines all the time?"

"I just don't want you imposing," said Mrs. Fenton. "That's all."

The following week they cooked omelettes.

"I'll show you special ones, like we did at school. It's really quite simple . . . all you have to do is break the eggs into a bowl the same as last time, except that instead of putting the whole lot in, you have to separate the yolks from the whites and whip the whites up by themselves. Look"—she passed him the special separating cup she had brought up with her from the kitchen—"this is what you use. It's a bit like a tea strainer. If you feel it, you'll see it's got a slit in the side. That's where the white goes through. Right? So, you let the white go into a cup, and then you pour it into the bowl—here you are." She took his hand. "Here's the bowl—and here's the cup—and these are the eggs, and you know how to crack them—"

"Yes, but not how to divide them into two! Marianne, I don't think I'm going to be able to manage omelettes."

"Of course you are. Don't be so feeble. It's the simplest

thing on earth . . . come on, I'll show you. Take this"—she thrust an egg into his hand—"and put the strainer on top of the cup—right?—and break the egg—like this—and then swizzle it round a bit, and there you are, you see, it's happening, the white's going out of the side and the rest's staying behind. Feel it—go on! With your finger—it won't hurt you, it's only sticky. Try tipping it this way a bit—that's it! Now all you've got left is the yolk. It's all so simple."

It may have seemed simple to her—she could appreciate perfectly that it was not so to Abe. It was a question, she thought, of making him feel things. Not just telling him what to do, but actually guiding him while he did it. That way he would get the pattern of it. She was quite triumphant when finally he succeeded in separating an egg all by himself, without any help whatsoever from her.

"You see?" she said. "You *see?*"

"Yes," he said. "I think maybe I've got the hang of it at last. Mind you, I should have, the way you've been haranguing me . . . haven't been so bullied and bossed since I was at nursery school being taught how to do my shoelaces up!"

She looked at him doubtfully. She hadn't meant to bully him—only teach him how to make an omelette. Had she perhaps been too high-handed? He was quite a lot older than she was. Maybe he didn't care to be pushed about and told what to do by a sixteen-year-old schoolgirl.

She remained subdued throughout the rest of the procedure. Abe noticed it. He said, "Come on, Marianne! What's the matter? Why have you stopped being masterful?"

"I thought I was being bossy."

"Well, good God, if you weren't, I'd still be dining off cold bread and butter, wouldn't I? Don't apologize for bossing me. It's exactly what I need."

She wished she could believe him; she couldn't quite be
sure. Over the omelettes, as they sat opposite each other at
the small, plastic-topped table, she said, "Abe . . . am I imposing?"

He responded promptly: "Very imposing! Don't fish for
compliments!"

"No. Seriously. You said you wanted to be independent—"

"So I did—and so I do. But that needn't stop me accepting
help gracefully." He stretched out a hand across the table,
feeling for hers. "I am very grateful. You do know that, don't
you? It's not everyone would go to all this trouble."

Marianne, crimson, said, "It isn't any trouble. I enjoy it."

"It must take up a lot of your time, though . . . all the
things you do for me."

"Doesn't matter. Haven't got much else to do anyway."

Abe was silent a moment, then: "Don't you ever go out
anywhere, Marianne?"

"Sometimes."

"Where do you go to?"

"Places."

"What places? Youth clubs? Discos?"

She made a grunting noise, vague and embarrassed.

"Movies?"

"Sometimes."

"What about weekends? What do you do then?"

"Shopping. Reading. Out on my bike."

"All by yourself?"

"Well—" She speared a chunk of omelette. "Mostly."

"You don't by any chance happen to sing, I suppose?"

"*Sing?*" She stared at him. "No, why?"

"Just that I'm always on the look-out for people who can.

I've got this group going—madrigals, lute songs, that kind of thing. Meets every Thursday. Of course, it might not be your scene, but I just thought, if you had any sort of voice at all . . ."

"I haven't," she said. She asserted it with glum certainty. Her voice was so incontestably awful that she hadn't even bothered auditioning for the school choir. Whenever she so much as opened her mouth, Miss Pargeter had clapped her hands to her ears with a querulous "Goes through one's head like a hacksaw." She said wistfully, "I wish I could—sing, I mean."

"Are you really so certain that you can't?"

"Really and utterly." Couldn't sing, couldn't dance, couldn't play the piano, couldn't do *anything*. And now she knew where it was that Abe went on Thursdays. Why for heaven's sake did she have to be so useless?

"What about boyfriends?" said Abe. "I'll bet you've got boyfriends."

The tide of crimson, which had started to recede, now came flooding back in full force. Down over her neck it washed, up over her forehead. She was glad, at that moment, that Abe couldn't see her.

"Not exactly . . . *boy*friends," she said. "That is—I mean —I *know* lots of boys, it's just that—that one doesn't want to get oneself tied down."

Abe agreed gravely that to get tied down would be folly indeed. Of course he knew that she had been telling the most atrocious lies. Even if he couldn't see the state of her face, it must be obvious. To cover the embarrassment, she said, "Have you?"

"Got a boyfriend?"

The embarrassment increased.

"*Girl* friend."

"Oh!" said Abe. "Girl friend . . . well, no, but then I don't find it that easy."

She glanced at him, automatically suspicious, but he didn't seem to be poking fun. He seemed quite serious. She thought of the Rosemount girl with the face of a Madonna.

"What about your pupils?" she said.

"Schoolgirls?" said Abe. "At my advanced age?"

"You're not as old as all that!"

Her mother would have said that that was impertinence. Abe didn't appear to think so. He only twitched an eyebrow and said, "Aren't I? So how old would you say?"

"Oh—" She hesitated. People were funny about their ages. When someone had asked Miss Jones, in all innocence, if she remembered the war, she had been quite glacial. "I may seem pretty ancient," she had said, "but I am not actually out of the ark. For your information, I had not even been *thought* of during the war." On the other hand, when Tip, at the age of fifteen (being somewhat of a midget) had been taken for two years younger, she had been even more outraged than Miss Jones. She wouldn't want to upset Abe by wildly over- or underestimating.

"Well?" he said. "Go on! Be brave! Hazard a guess."

"Oh . . . twenties?" she said. She couldn't go far wrong with that.

Abe jeered. "Playing it safe? What do you want? A decade either way?"

"Well, I don't suppose you remember the war?" she said.

"No, I do not! I don't remember horse-drawn vehicles, either."

"Steam trains?"

He choked. "How about silent movies and crystal sets

while you're at it? As a matter of fact, I missed the coronation by about eighteen months—and don't ask me *which* coronation!"

Demurely, she said, "George the Fifth, I suppose?"

She worked it out that he was twenty-four and a bit. It did sound quite old until you got it in perspective—until you stopped to think that it was only *eight* years older than sixteen (actually seven and a half, because before he was twenty-five she would have had a birthday and caught up) and that by the time you got to, say, sixty and seventy and eighty you were so far gone that it really didn't make any difference, because by then the years simply telescoped. She explained as much to Abe, but he only laughed.

"I still don't think Miss Halliday would take very kindly to the idea of my making advances to any of her girls!"

Miss Halliday was the headmistress up at Rosemount—a dragon, from all accounts, and a puritanical one at that. Miss Halliday would certainly never countenance the giving of an Easter party with boys on the premises. There was something, Marianne thought, to having a puritan for headmistress. It must be hard on Abe, though. Surrounded by all those beautiful willowy Rosemounters and not able to do anything about it. She regarded him with solemn sympathy.

"Haven't you got a girl friend at all?"

That was more impertinence. Abe grinned. "*Oy vay!* Bring on the violins . . . I did have one, once, believe it or not."

She believed it. Why shouldn't she? She didn't suppose that Abe told lies like she did—he wouldn't need to. He could talk to people and get on with people. She bet there were dozens of his pupils who wouldn't mind going out with him.

"What happened to her?" she said. "Your girl friend?"

Cheerfully, Abe chased the last piece of omelette around

his plate, resorting in the end, without shame, to the use of fingers.

"She went off on a skiing holiday and came back with someone else."

"She went off *without* you?"

"Well, I wouldn't be much use on a pair of skis, would I?"

"Then why did she go?"

"I suppose she fancied the idea."

"Well, she oughtn't to have done!"

"Oughtn't she?" said Abe.

"No, she oughtn't!" Marianne was emphatic. "She ought to have chosen something you could both do."

"Like walking over the South Downs with a guide dog and a bottle of brandy?" He smiled. "She wasn't the type. In any case, you could hardly expect her to curtail her activities just because of me."

"Why not?"

"Oh . . . things don't work that way. Why should she?"

Marianne could think of a hundred reasons. "I wouldn't have gone," she said.

"Wouldn't you? No, perhaps you wouldn't. You're a very caring sort of person, though, aren't you?"

Again her cheeks glowed. Am I? she thought. Was she? She only wished Miss Jones might hear it.

"It's not being *caring*," she said, "it's being fair."

"Well, whatever it is . . . to be perfectly honest, I think the poor girl was growing just a little bit tired of having to drag me along everywhere by the hand and do things for me. That was when I decided to make a bid for independence—been spoon-fed too long. You're working wonders, incidentally. Do you realize that a few weeks ago I could scarcely even boil an egg? Now I can crack them and beat them and separate them into two and even make omelettes out of them!"

He expected her to smile, but she didn't. She was too busy brooding over this so-called girl friend of his, who had deserted him in order to go skiing and had come back with someone else.

"What was her name?" she said.

"Gretta. Why?"

"She sounds hateful."

"She wasn't hateful. Just a normal girl who wanted to enjoy herself in the normal way."

Marianne said stubbornly, "*I* think she sounds hateful. She shouldn't have started going out with you in the first place if she wasn't prepared to—" She paused, wondering how to say it.

"If she wasn't prepared to put up with me being useless?"

"No! If she wasn't prepared to—well—make allowances."

"Oh, she made allowances . . . it just got a bit boring, that's all. I think it embarrassed her."

"*Embarrassed* her?"

"Having me tagging along at her side like a pet dog."

"Well, really!" said Marianne. (It seemed convenient to forget that just at the beginning it had embarrassed her as well. After all, she had conquered it very quickly. It certainly didn't embarrass her now.) "What on earth," she said scornfully, "is there to be embarrassed about?"

"I don't know," said Abe, "but people are. It upsets them. It makes them feel awkward."

Had he ever guessed that it had made her feel awkward? That first day, taking him to the bus—her arm like a ramrod, stiff, not moving—

"It doesn't make Sarah feel awkward, does it?" she said.

"Oh, Sarah! She's grown up with it . . . she was walking me halfway around London when she was still only knee-high to a milk bottle. You can't judge other people by Sarah."

No, thought Marianne. Sarah was everything that was marvelous. Sarah was the cat's whiskers. Don't judge anyone by Sarah.

"It doesn't embarrass *me*," she said.

"No," said Abe. "That's why you're good for me . . . you push me around and make me do things. And talking of doing things—" He rapped with his finger on the table. "Time we stopped maundering. Get yourself over to that piano stool; it's my turn now to be boss—and I give you due warning, I can bully just as well as you can!"

8

>>>

THE DAY ARRIVED—THE INEVITABLE DAY—WHEN BETH
Walker wanted money for the party.

"Come on, Fenton! Stump up! Two quid you owe me."

"Yes—" Marianne looked in her purse, though she already
knew perfectly well what was there: one pound ten pence to
last her the rest of the week. "Can I give it to you Monday?"

Beth narrowed her eyes. "You are still coming?"

"Course she's still coming!"

"She's bringing her boyfriend—"

"The one who's a musician—"

"The concert pianist—"

"Alan—"

"Adam—"

"Adam?"

"*Well?*" said Beth. "*Are* you?"

"Look, it's just that I'm broke," said Marianne. "I'll let you
have it first thing, I promise."

"No, I mean . . . are you still coming?"

"And are you still bringing the boyfriend?"

"The concert pianist—"

"The musician—"

Goaded, she snapped, "No, I'm bringing a cardboard cut-
out! You'll just have to wait and see, won't you?"

That night in bed she lay and sweated. Between the beginning of the term and the end, anything might have happened (except that it hadn't); between now and Monday there seemed no conceivable chance. Between Monday and the following Saturday—her cheek against the pillow glowed red hot. She would have to hand over the money. She could think of no way of getting out of it. It would be two pounds thrown down the drain, but better that than they should suspect.

They would suspect anyhow. They would do more than suspect: they would know. Even if she did pay the money— even if she contrived by some miracle to throw herself down the stairs at the last minute and break her leg—when she didn't turn up, they would know. There would be looks exchanged and leering grimaces—nodding of heads and loud proclamations of having "said so all along." Mary-Jane Mountain would be the loudest of them all.

"Musician! She doesn't know any musician!"

"But I do!" Marianne sat up, clutching at the bedclothes. "I *do*!"

She knew Abe, didn't she? What was he, if not a musician? After all, *she* had never said he was a concert pianist. That had been the Rivers-Smith, stupid cow. Marianne had not made any such extravagant claims. Of course, she had told them that he was called Adam, but she could always pretend they had misheard, and really he wasn't as old as all that, not so old that people would think it ludicrous, and if she could only persuade him into wearing dark glasses and leaving his stick behind, then maybe nobody would notice, nobody would realize—you couldn't tell just from looking at him. Not if he wore dark glasses. And she would give him her word, she wouldn't leave his side, not for an instant; she wouldn't let him get lost or bump into things. It wasn't as if he would have to dance, or do anything he couldn't manage. They need only stay a short while—just long enough to be seen. She would say they had to go on somewhere else, somewhere more adult. Surely he wouldn't mind, just for one evening?

She threw back the covers, snatched up her bathrobe. It was eleven o'clock at night and her mother would have a fit, but if she didn't do it now she knew she never would. Leave it till morning and she would be too appalled by her own audacity even to consider the idea.

"Abe—" She tapped at his door, very low. "It's me—Marianne. Can I come in?"

She opened the door the tiniest crack. The room was in darkness. For just a second she thought he must be asleep, but then he said, "Sounds to me as if you already are!" and switched on the light. She saw that he had been sitting up in bed with one of the big volumes of Braille that he kept on the bedside table.

Sidetracked, she said, "Abe, how ever do you read from those things?"

"Sh!" He put a finger to his lips. "I'll show you one day. Not now. What's up? Can't you sleep?"

"I wanted to ask you something. I wanted to—"

"Hadn't you better shut the door? You don't want to wake your mother."

No. She could imagine the tirade: "Going into a guest's room at eleven o'clock at night—" Going into a *man's* room, in her pajamas. Not that Abe could see she was in her pajamas. She closed the door and, standing at the foot of the bed, said very quickly, "You wouldn't like to come to a party, would you?"

"A party?" He seemed surprised. "What sort of a party?"
"Easter one. At school. Next Saturday."

Abe was silent. Marianne gripped the bedrail with both hands.

"It's not a kids' thing. It's only for the senior high. Everyone's bringing a boyfriend or a—a brother, or a cousin, or something. I thought . . . perhaps . . . you might enjoy it."

Still Abe remained silent. He doesn't want to, she thought. He's got better things to do. He goes up to his sister's. He sees Sarah Lawrence, and she takes him around London. Why should he want to give that up only for the sake of some tinpot little party?

Confused, she backed away toward the door.

"I—I just wondered," she said. "I wasn't sure. I—"

"Marianne." Marking his place with one hand, Abe held out the other. Uncertainly, she stopped. "It's not that I wouldn't like to, but . . . I'm not terribly clever at that sort of thing. Parties, dancing—I can't even dance. I wouldn't be very much credit to you."

"Yes, you would!" she said. And then, in case that sounded too eager: "I can't dance, either—I mean, not properly. Not waltzing and all that stuff. But I don't think they do nowadays. I think they just sort of move about on the spot marking time."

"Ah." There was a pause. "I suppose even I could manage to do that," said Abe.

"Yes, and we wouldn't have to stay long—not if you didn't want to. If you wanted to go up to your sister's, I could always see you on to the train and—"

"Really, Marianne!" Abe put a marker in his book and closed it up. "What do you take me for? Some kind of a lout?

I thought it was still the custom, even in this age of enlightenment, for the gentleman to see the lady home. Or am I hopelessly behind the times?"

She was never quite certain, with Abe, whether he was teasing her or not. She hadn't meant to insult him. It was only that it would be perfectly simple for her to walk up to the station with him and put him on a train and then go back out and catch the bus. She didn't want him to miss out on the whole of his weekend; not just for her. It wouldn't be right. She tried to explain, but he cut her short. "For heaven's sake! As if I can't survive a single weekend without rushing back to the nest. If one goes to a party, one goes to a party. . . . I don't get invited to all that many. Let me at least make the most of it while I can!"

"You mean"—she hardly dared say it—"you really would like to come?"

"Certainly I should really like to come. I'm very flattered to be asked. Next Saturday, did you say?"

"Yes." Joyfully, she moved back into the room. "It starts at seven thirty. It finishes about eleven. Everyone has to be off the premises by then. Some of the staff will be there, but they never interfere. They just sit it out in the staff room guzzling gin. Not that *we're* allowed gin, but—"

"Not to worry," said Abe. "I'm not a gin addict."

"I think there may be cider. I don't really know." She had not, until now, been sufficiently interested to find out. Quite suddenly, the party had ceased to be a blot on the horizon. There were actually rays of sunshine peering through the clouds. "I think it might be quite fun," she said.

"Of course it will be fun! You must tell me what you want me to wear."

"Oh, just jeans and sweater, the same as usual. There isn't any need to get dressed up, and—and you won't really need to bring your stick with you, will you? Not just for a party? There's hardly anywhere to walk, except up to the bus stop, and you know that like the back of your hand, and I *shall* be there with you, so—"

Her tone, perhaps, had been more anxious than she intended. Abe smiled very slightly and said: "I can leave it behind, if you wish—*if* you're willing to take the responsibility for me."

"I will! I promise! I give you my word! I wouldn't let anything happen to you."

"I'm quite sure you wouldn't . . . but, Marianne—" Again, he stretched out a hand. This time, because she was closer, it encountered hers. He took it for just a second. Gently he said, "They'll still know."

She swallowed. "Kn-know?"

"There really isn't any way of disguising it. I would if I could, but—"

Agitated, she snatched her hand away. "I don't want you d-disguising anything! It wasn't that! I just thought it would be easier for you—for d-dancing and holding d-drinks and everything."

"For moving about on the spot marking time, and everything?"

"Yes! I thought it would be easier! I'm not like *her*. It doesn't *embarrass* me."

"Hush," said Abe. "You'll wake your mother."

"Well, but I wouldn't have invited you if it did, would I?"

"No, you wouldn't," he said. "Are you quite sure you still want to?"

"Of c-course I still want to!" She was suddenly stricken by a renewal of doubt. "If you still want to c-come, that is."

"I still want to come."

"And you w-*will* trust me to take care of you?"

"No sweat," said Abe.

She ought to have felt triumphant, but somehow she did not.

She had known instinctively that there was going to be trouble about taking Abe to the party, just as there had been about the piano lessons. She wasn't in the least surprised when one evening over supper her mother said, "What's all this I hear about you asking Mr. Shonfeld to go to a party with you?"

"I asked him if he'd like to and he said yes."

"You mean, you asked him if he *would* and he didn't like to say no."

"He could have said no if that's what he wanted. . . . He doesn't get invited to all that many parties."

"Neither do you."

She looked up, surprised and indignant. What had she done to provoke that particular piece of malice? As a rule her mother was not so waspish.

"It's a school thing," she said.

"I know it's a school thing. I should have thought Mr. Shonfeld had more than enough of school things during the week, without being dragged into them at weekends as well."

"Nobody's dragging him, he—"

"Just because he turned out not to be so ancient as you anticipated, that doesn't mean you have the right to commandeer him."

"I am not *commandeering* him! He didn't have to come!"

"No, and you didn't have to ask him . . . putting him in an awkward position."

"As a matter of fact"—nonchalantly, Marianne stirred sugar into her tea—"he *thanked* me for asking him."

"Of course he thanked you! He's a very well brought up young man. What did you expect him to do? Turn around and tell you outright to stop bothering him?"

Marianne flushed. "Abe's not like that."

"I'm perfectly well aware that he's not like that. It's the very reason why I wish you hadn't asked him. You shouldn't have had to ask him, in any case. You ought to know someone of your own."

She scowled. "Fat chance! Where do I ever get to meet *someone of my own?* You think anybody around here wants to know me? Going to the snob school? If you'd sent me to Hillside the same as—"

"There's nothing to stop you joining somewhere. There's a perfectly good church youth club."

"Church youth club!" They had had all this out before. It had been Miss Pargeter's constant parrot cry: That girl isn't normal . . . why can't she *join* things?

"And what, pray," said Mrs. Fenton, "is wrong with the church youth club?"

Her lip curled contemptuously. "Nothing but organized walks and Ping-Pong."

"So what do you expect? Organized pot and gang-bangs?"

"Anything's better than organized *walks*—great cretinous hordes stomping all over the country. . . . Anyway, I don't go to church."

"It might do you good if you did. What time does this party, or whatever it is, finish?"

"*I* don't know. Could go on till midnight."

"So how are you supposed to get home?"

"Bus. Walk. Taxi. What does it matter? I'll be with Abe." She banged her cup down angrily onto its saucer. "He is a *man*, you know. He may be blind, but he's perfectly capable of taking care of me."

"He shouldn't have to take care of you. He's got a life of his own to lead—he doesn't want to spend all his spare time escorting schoolgirls to parties. In future you wait until he asks you."

"Oh, in future I'll just sit by the fire and *knit*! I sometimes wonder," Marianne said bitterly, "whatever happened to Women's Lib. . . . It stands about as much chance in this house as a black man in the Ku Klux Klan!"

Next morning, on the way to the bus stop, Abe said: "You're very silent—like the first day all over again! I could understand it, then. You were scared of me, weren't you?"

"No, I wasn't!"

"Yes, you were! Scared rigid! But you're not anymore. What's wrong? Problems at school?"

She had noticed before that he was sensitive to her moods. He couldn't actually see that she had a frown on her face, but he always knew. She muttered, "It's her."

"Who's her?"

"My mother. Always going on at me—always fussing and bothering. Always *some*thing."

"Oh! Is that all?" He sounded remarkably cheerful about it. "Doesn't everybody's?"

She looked up at him, struck suddenly by what was for her a totally novel idea. "Did yours?"

"You'd better believe it!"

How strange. She had never thought of Abe as having a mother—not in the sense of a mother who fussed and bothered and wielded power. Abe was grown up. Grownups didn't have to contend with that sort of thing.

"I wouldn't *mind,*" she said, "if she didn't go *on* so."

"What does she go on about?"

"You mostly . . . how I impose on you. How I shouldn't have asked you to come with me on Saturday. How it's not your job in life to escort *school*girls."

There was a pause. Then Abe said, "Would she rather I didn't?"

"She'd rather I hadn't asked. *She* thinks you'd like to have told me where to put myself only that you've been too well brought up and you're too nice and you don't want to hurt my feelings. It's you she's worried about, not me. She thinks you're being put upon."

"Would it help if I were to reassure her?"

"Only if you really meant it."

"And *don't* you think I really mean it?"

"I—I'm not absolutely p-positive."

"Well, be absolutely positive! When I say I'm flattered, I'm flattered. It's not as if I receive invitations to parties every day of the week—there aren't so many people would be prepared to take the trouble."

Her cheeks fired up. She had never been prone to blushing when she was younger. The older she grew, the worse it seemed to become—and worst of all when she was with Abe, which was really quite ridiculous when he couldn't even see her.

"It isn't any trouble," she said.

"Isn't it? I should say it was a great deal—promising to be responsible for me."

She fiddled for a bit with the strap of her briefcase. "Actually, I've—I've been thinking about that. I think maybe you —you ought to take your stick after all. Not because I don't *want* to be responsible—I mean, I won't go off and leave you, or anything—but . . . well . . . suppose I suddenly had a heart attack in the street or dropped down dead or something? You'd be lost, wouldn't you? If you didn't have it?"

"It wouldn't be easy," he said, gravely, "but since I don't for one minute anticipate that you *will* have a heart attack or drop down dead—"

"No, but I—I still think you ought to take it. I think you'd feel happier." She scanned his face earnestly. "You would, wouldn't you?"

"It's entirely up to you," said Abe. "It's your scene— they're your people."

"Well, then—I think you ought to take it." What did she care what they thought? She wasn't ashamed of him—she wasn't another Gretta.

"I'll tell you what," said Abe. "We can always abandon it for moving about on the spot."

9

MRS. FENTON, BREAKING RULES FOR ONCE, SAID THAT IF ABE
were giving up his weekend "just to escort you to a party,
then the least we can do is make sure he's fed properly.
You'd better tell him to come down and have dinner with
us—or perhaps I'd better."

"No, I'll do it," said Marianne. "I'll tell him."

"Well, make sure that he comes. Tell him I insist."

At first, when she knocked at his door and said, "Abe!
You're to come down and have dinner with us," he seemed
reluctant.

"Really," he said, "there's no need. I can manage."

Marianne, thinking it was his precious independence that
he was worried about, said, "Once isn't going to compromise
you. Anyway, you've got to, she insists. It's her way of satis-
fying her conscience about you taking me out this evening."

"Oh, but that's ridiculous! I'm quite happy to take you
out."

"Yes, *I* know that"—growing confidence made her cheeky,
but Abe never minded—"it's her that doesn't."

"Well, I'll tell her."

"She'll still say you've got to come and eat with us . . . why don't you want to? She's doing a proper three-course dinner in your honor."

Only after much probing and prompting did she finally succeed in dragging the truth from him. Shamefaced he muttered, "I never feel my table manners are up to eating three-course dinners in company."

"Oh, *Abe*," she said; and then, in case his feelings had been hurt: "What on earth do you think is wrong with your table manners?"

Abe screwed up his face and said, "You should ask? You've had to sit and watch me often enough."

"Well, but no one minds if you knock things over. I do it all the time."

"It's not knocking things over."

"Then—" She wrinkled her brow in genuine perplexity. She herself was used to the torment of secret doubts and fears; but Abe? She thought back over the meals they had eaten together and still she couldn't see what it was that bothered him, unless perhaps it was the fact that just occasionally, when food was being more than usually tiresome, he used fingers; and really it was difficult to imagine how that could ever upset anyone. It had never upset her. Why shouldn't he use fingers, if that was what came easiest to him? *She* had tried keeping her eyes shut tight and chasing bits of food round her plate with knife and fork. It was even more frustrating than that stupid game where you had to shake metal balls into little holes. The wonder of it was that he should be able to manage as well as he did. "You've never minded with me," she said.

"That's because you're you. I don't count you as company."

"Well, you can hardly count my mother as company. You eat breakfast in front of her every morning."

"Breakfast is different. Everyone's in too much of a hurry to notice at breakfast."

"So no one's going to notice at dinner, because there isn't anything *to* notice . . . honestly. I mean it. Just so long as you don't put your elbows on the table. She's got a thing about elbows on the table. Says it's uncouth. God knows why. What are tables for? All so *point*less. Like gentlemen raising hats and walking on the outside, and anyway, why gentlemen? Why should *they* be the ones to have to get mud on themselves? It's like 'innocent women and children' in time of war, and 'British mothers' whenever there's disaster . . . just *clap*trap."

By degrees she coaxed him into it—"But only so long as you apologize for me in advance"—and in any event it was she, not Abe, who sent the contents of the water pitcher shooting over the table. He said afterward, accusingly, on the bus, "Did you do that on purpose? Just to make me feel better?" She denied it with what vehemence she could, but plainly he was not convinced. She supposed there wasn't any way of ever making him believe that by nature she was a thousand times more clumsy than he.

They arrived at the party twenty minutes late, because of the buses not running on time. She couldn't have planned it better had she tried. It was obvious, from the looks on people's faces as she walked in, that they had already satisfied themselves she wasn't coming. Mary-Jane Mountain, towing her second Laurence Olivier (who didn't look in the least like Olivier but more a contender for Humpty Dumpty) said, "Oh! You're here!" in accents that quite gave the game away.

"Did you think I wouldn't be?" said Marianne; and then, very quickly, before there should be any mistakes: "This is Abe."

"Abe?" said Mary-Jane. "I thought you said—"

"Abe, this is Mary-Jane, who's in the same class as me, and Barry, who's at R.A.D.A."

Barry, with hearty affability, said, "Hi."

Mary-Jane said: "Are you a musician?"

"Sorry?" said Abe.

"I told you," said Marianne. "He plays the piano."

"Oh, musician!" said Abe. "I thought for a moment you said magician!"

"Sloppy diction," said Barry.

Mary-Jane, obviously confused, only made a foolish scraping noise in the back of her throat. It did one good to see the great hectoring Mountain for once at a loss. She didn't even try asking him if he were a concert pianist.

Just to begin with, Mary-Jane was not the only one to be at a loss. There was a definite tendency on the part of almost everyone present to skirt, as it were, around the edges. Marianne would catch people looking nervously at Abe, when they thought she wasn't watching, and then when they found that she was, they would instantly fall to bobbing and beaming and nodding with their heads and grinning sheepish grins indicative of goodwill. She knew that first thing Monday morning there were going to be buzzing sessions. So what? If they'd never seen a blind person before, that was their problem. She was glad she hadn't tried to make Abe wear dark glasses and leave his stick behind. It would have seemed like cheating, and it would have branded her as no better than Gretta, who had gone skiing without him and been ashamed to take him places.

While she was in the washroom, Meg Munroe, who was one of the Mountain's bosom buddies, came in and smiled at her, in quite a friendly fashion but just a trifle reproachfully, and said, "You ought to have told us, you know. We'd have understood."

"Understood what?" said Marianne. As if she weren't very well aware.

"About your boyfriend. He teaches up at Rosemount, doesn't he?"

She stiffened, jerking at the roller towel. "So?"

"I've got a cousin who goes there . . . I wondered why she'd suddenly started piano lessons when she's practically tone deaf!"

Marianne, frowning sternly into the roller towel to quell gratification, said, "He does take them for class things as well as private."

"Wouldn't you know it? And here are we, stuck with old Organ Morgan . . . talk about some people having all the luck. Hey, I bet my cousin turns green when I tell her, though! Fancy picking on you when he could have had the whole of Rosemount!"

She supposed that in a way it was a sort of compliment, except, of course, that Abe hadn't picked on her. If anything, she'd picked on him.

She looked at her face in the cracked washroom mirror. No denying it, her mouth *was* too large, and her nose *was* a funny shape, and she *did* have freckles all over. The only comfort to be derived was that at least Abe couldn't know.

She went back to the hall to find that the old school record player had broken down—Miss Morgan wouldn't allow them to use the proper hi-fi set up from the music room, she said they would blow the speakers out, playing pop—and that Abe was being dragged across to the piano by an overexcited member of the junior class. She heard Emily Rivers-Smith's voice, shrill and self-righteous: "He's a concert pianist—you can't ask a *concert* pianist. Marianne, tell them! They can't ask him to play *their* crapulous stuff!"

"Perhaps he offered," she said.

"He didn't offer! They pressganged him!"

"Well . . . I suppose he could have said no."

Would he have said no? No, he probably wouldn't. He would think that obliging them in an emergency was what she would want him to do. It *was* what she would want him to do, except—except that she had only ever heard him play strictly classical. She dug her nails hard into the palms of her hands. Please, Abe, she thought, don't make it Mozart.

He didn't make it Mozart. It seemed he was perfectly capable, after all, of descending to less exalted spheres when occasion demanded. Emily Rivers-Smith sniffed and said, "It's *rubbish*. He ought to be playing heavenly beautiful Beethoven, not demeaning himself."

"Heavenly beautiful Beethoven," said Marianne, "would be like feeding donkeys strawberries."

People stopped skirting around the edges now that Abe was playing the piano. Instead, they jostled at his elbow saying super, smashing, great—hey! Do you know that one that goes like this? She might almost have begun to grow resentful, except that somebody or other's spotty boyfriend, who was good with his hands, finally managed to get the record player going again so that Abe could be released.

"Demeaning yourself," she said.

"Prostituting my art."

"*I* didn't know you could play that sort of stuff."

"Didn't know that I could slum it?" He grinned. "One

doesn't, as a rule—one is, after all, supposed to be a respectable music master with a sense of responsibility. Makes a pleasant change to be able to let one's hair down."

Marianne, nodding graciously, like royalty, in the direction of the Mountain, squirming Uriah˙Heap-ish appreciation from the other side of the hall, said: "Gave *them* something to think about."

"Do I detect a note of smugness? Don't get too puffed up . . . that sort of stuff is mere child's play. If I could rattle off the Liszt Sonata in B with the same careless rapture, we might have cause for congratulation."

She didn't know anything about the Liszt Sonata in B, but hazarding a guess she said, "Bet you couldn't dance to it, though."

"Possibly not. Do you want to, by the way?"

"Dance?"

"It sounds as if everyone else is."

She gazed about her. Certainly a number of people were in rather hectic motion. She watched them awhile, and there didn't seem to be any particular rules about it. No one, as far as she could see, was doing any set steps. While some flung themselves about like creatures demented, others, with ritual solemnity, simply gyrated on the spot.

"I suppose we could always try," she said.

"Well, don't sound so dubious! If I'm willing to give it a go, surely you ought to be?"

Dancing was easier than she had thought. Abe held her very close, as of course he had to, adrift in all that sea of humanity and in an unfamiliar place, and after a bit, when she had stopped being embarrassed, she let her head rest on his shoulder, and she thought: "This is me—Mari*anne*." And she could hardly quite believe it even now. The Easter party and she there, with Abe—dancing with him, close to him, for all the world as if he really were the boyfriend that she had told them he was. Already, in her head, she was composing letters: *Dear Tip, Last week it was the party and I went with Abe. I can't remember if I told you about Abe. He's Jewish and he's a musician and has this gorgeous profile like Rudolph Valentino.* (She couldn't claim that his eyes were blue or that he had "the most fantastic suntan," but at any rate being a Jewish musician was more romantic than being a New Zealand sheep shearer any day of the week.) *The Mountain, needless to say, is absolutely* CONSUMED. (*Laurence Olivier turns out to be plump and pasty. After all that buildup! ! !*) *We spent practically the* ENTIRE EVENING *dancing together, and everyone—*

"Have you got your eyes open?" said Abe.

"Yes!" she said. She opened them, quickly. Jo Dyer from the junior class, gyrating nearby with a strange, pale youth actually wearing a school blazer, wagged a finger at her in mock reproof. Across the room, the Mountain was grinning. She tossed her head. Let her grin! What did she care? For the first time ever, she was conscious of superiority. Pimpled spawn, that's all that lot were. Spotty cheeks and blazers. At least Abe was *mature*. Once upon a time, only a few days back, she had wished with all her heart that the Easter party might be over and done with and safely behind them. Now, as she heard the nearby church clock strike eleven, she felt like Cinderella at the ball. Allowing them some leeway, it was ten minutes past when Miss Cooper (*"Sozzled,"* said the Mountain, the following week. "Positively plastered, *je vous donne ma parole"*) finally put her head around the door and announced: "Time, ladies and gentlemen, please." She wished it might have been Miss Jones rather than the Coop.

She would have liked Miss Jones to have seen her there, with Abe. Perhaps the Coop might mention it—just in passing would do. Something along the lines of: "By the way, did you know that Marianne Fenton turned up on Saturday, after all? With a concert pianist, so I'm told. . . ." Probably she wouldn't, but it was nice to speculate.

They didn't take the bus home, because Abe said it wasn't fitting. He said they should go up to the station and grab themselves a cab. She wished he could have seen, as they walked through the nighttime streets, that the moon was up and the sky full of stars. It seemed only right that it should be so. She tried telling him, and obligingly he raised his head and said, "Is the Plow up there? The Plow's the only one I can recognize." She said that it was, and Orion's Belt, as well, and he said, "Ah, yes. That's another one . . . three in the middle and one at either end"; but it wasn't the same as being able to see for himself.

She wondered, as they walked, if he ever had. Surely he must have? He couldn't have been born blind. People weren't; not nowadays. It was something that only happened through accidents or when you got old. Timidly, she said: "Abe, did you—"

"Did I what?"

"Did you . . . have an accident?"

"Accident?"

"I mean . . . you haven't always—"

"Always been like I am now?" He squeezed her arm, reassuringly. "It's all right, I don't mind you asking. The answer is yes: always."

"Right from—when you were little?"

"Right from the very time when I was born. Can't get much littler than that."

She was awed into silence. It was something, she thought, that was beyond comprehension—beyond the powers of ordinary imagining. Never to have seen the sun come up over the hills in the early morning, or sink like a great blood-red ball beyond the rooftops at night; never to have seen birds or flowers or trees—never to have seen *people*. Never, in the whole of his life, to have seen anything at all. How could he know, when she said the stars were shining, what stars were really like? How could you describe them to him? Little silver dots that twinkle? But what was silver? What was twinkle? What pictures could he have in his head if never in all his life, from the very time that he was born—

"Tell me," said Abe. "What do you usually do on Sundays?"

With an effort, she pulled herself back. "Go out on my bike, as a rule. Into the country."

"Real country?"

"Well—" She was cautious. "Depends what you mean by real country."

"Cows, horses . . . that kind of thing."

"Oh, it's got cows and horses. Got pigs and chickens as well, if it comes to that. *And* foxes—watch out for the steps, we're coming to the underpass—*and* rabbits. *And* badgers, if you know where to look for them."

Abe waited until the steps had been safely negotiated, then said, "I've never been to the country. Not real country. Not cows-and-horses-and-pigs sort of country."

She stared at him, shocked. "*Never?* Not even for holidays?"

"We always went abroad." He said it apologetically. "Venice, Rome, Florence . . . my mother has this mad passion for Italy. I suppose"—he hesitated—"if I were to ask to come with you—would it be a great nuisance?"

Come with her? Into the country? Into the *Kingdom*? Her immediate reaction was that it wasn't feasible. The way was too tortuous. How could he cope with puddles and potholes and barbed-wire fences when even ordinary roads presented difficulties? And then she thought: *But he's asked me—he's actually* ASKED *me.* Shyly she said, "Would you really like to?"

"Only if it's not going to be a nuisance."

"It wouldn't be a nuisance," she said.

"But how would we get there? I can't ride a bicycle."

"That's all right, we can always go by bus. Green line—only takes twenty minutes."

"You're sure I won't slow things up?"

What did it matter if he did? He had actually *asked* her. Teasing, more sure of herself, she said, "Won't be allowed to—I shall drag you unmercifully! Headfirst through the brambles . . . mind, it will be a bit boggy. You'll need some old shoes."

"I can find some old shoes. Just so long as you really are certain that I won't put a damper on things. You have to remember that I'm a soft city dweller . . . not used to treading real grass."

"Oh, it'll be more than just grass! It'll be mud and stiles and cowpats, and ditches full of dirty water, and—"

"You make it sound like an assault course," said Abe. "You don't think perhaps that I'm being a bit vainglorious?"

She did, as a matter of fact, have her doubts, but not for worlds would she let him suspect it. Firmly, as she piloted him across the road to the taxi stand, she said, "Don't go getting cold feet. You know you can rely on me. *I* won't let you fall into any heffalump traps or sit on any wasp nests."

Abe, in reply, only said: "Hm!"

In the cab that took them home he held her hand. He didn't try to kiss her. She wondered if it was because he didn't feel like kissing her or whether it was because he considered her too young. *For a girl of your age, you really are quite extraordinarily immature* . . . Suppose she had not been immature? Would he then?

She stood waiting for him by the front gate as he paid off the cab. The cab drove off. Abe said, "Marianne?"

"I'm here—"

He held out a hand. "Before we go in . . . I just wanted to say thank you. For a very lovely evening."

Perhaps *then*. Perhaps then was when he might have been going to do it. She would never know. The front door had opened and Mrs. Fenton was there on the step in her blue woolly bathrobe.

"I thought I heard a taxi . . . very extravagant! Very naughty. Have you had a good time?"

It was Abe, polite as always, who replied. "Extremely enjoyable." Marianne was too busy trying not to scream. She wished, just for once—she really did wish—that she could catch his eye and signal silent messages. Could Abe's mother ever, possibly, have been like hers? Had *she* hovered on doorsteps, not knowing when she wasn't wanted? Had *she* asked asinine questions, made futile remarks?

"I hope," said Mrs. Fenton, "that this daughter of mine has thanked you properly for taking her?"

Marianne's fingers curled in agony. Abe's hand over hers tightened its grip.

"The pleasure was entirely mine," he said.

10

>>>

"He asked me," said Marianne.

"Yes! All right! So you said! Just make sure you look after him, that's all. I don't want you taking him anywhere he can't manage. You seem to forget, it's not so easy for him—he can't go crashing about like an elephant, the way you do. I don't want you running off and leaving him to fend for himself."

"I *won't*."

"Well, don't. Just remember that you're responsible for him."

As if she needed to be told. She might be immature, but she wasn't an actual cretin. Leave him to fend for himself! It wasn't even what a ten-year-old would do. She grumbled to Abe about it all the way to the bus.

"Nothing but nag, nag. . . . Why does she have to go *on* so? She doesn't just make the point once, she makes it over and over until you feel like screaming."

"Mothers do. You probably will yourself one day."

"I probably *won't* myself one day . . . I shall remember only too vividly how it was when *I* was young."

Abe smiled slightly but said nothing.

"Don't do this, don't do that . . . what does she *think* I'm going to do? Abandon you in a field full of mangel-wurzels?"

"You'd better not!"

"Well, of *course* I won't. But you do want to see things, don't you?" She looked up at him, anxiously scanning his face. "You don't just want to keep to the beaten track?"

"Don't I?" said Abe. "No, I suppose I don't. That would be *very* feeble-minded of me. You take me wherever you feel like taking me. I don't mind if I'm gored to death by a herd of wild sheep or swallowed up in some noisome bog."

She took him the way she always went, up the lane by the side of the church, up the path through the woods, on past the chalk quarry, across the buttercup field. The path through the woods was boggy and winding, too narrow in places for them to walk side by side. Now and again, to avoid the worst of the mud, they were forced to leave the path and duck through the trees or clamber up on to the bank. Try as she might, it wasn't always possible to keep Abe from stepping in puddles or slipping on the squelchy ground, but he didn't seem to mind terribly. He said he'd come prepared for an assault course and couldn't very well complain if that was what he got. Ducking under the trees was the worst part. She held back all the branches that she could, but still it was slow going.

"It's not nearly so bad in summer," she said encouragingly. "You can stick to the path, then. Only takes half the time."

"I bet it only takes *you* half the time when you don't have me to drag along with you."

She couldn't deny it; but "What does it matter?" she said. "We've got all day—and after all, it is a new experience for you."

"Yes," he said, "it certainly is that!"

She asked him, as at last they came out again to clear

ground, whether he wanted a rest, but stoically he said no, they should press on to wherever it was they were going.

"I take it we have some objective in view?"

"Yes, but I'm not telling you till we get there. It's somewhere special—I've never taken anyone there before. You're the very first."

He squeezed her arm and said, "I'm flattered," as if he really meant it.

Along the chalk ridge, skirting the quarry, he kept stopping every few yards to say, "What's that?"—whereupon Marianne would stop too, and listen a moment, and say, "Just something in the hedge" or "Squirrels fighting" or "Woodpecker somewhere." Once, so intent was she on watching where Abe was treading, she forgot to look where she herself was putting her feet and narrowly avoided crushing an uncommonly large snail to death. She bent to pick him up. At once Abe said, "What's happening?"

"Nothing . . . hold out your hand. Tell me what this is."

"It's not going to be something horrid, is it?"

"What would be something horrid?"

"I don't know . . . snake?"

"Snakes aren't horrid, they're beautiful. Anyway, it's not a snake . . . come on! Take it!"

Abe, pulling a henpecked face, said: "Yes, miss."

"So what is it?"

"It's a—it's a snail, please, miss."

"Isn't he *vast*? And what about this?"

Darting suddenly into the hedgerow, she emerged triumphant with something else that had caught her eye. Abe fingered it dubiously.

"Don't know . . . what is it?"

"Old bird's nest. Not sure what sort. Something tiny. Feel how soft it is."

"Feels like a woolly pouch."

"Yes. Looks like one, a bit."

Taking Abe along the chalk ridge, identifying sounds, pointing things out to him—"Bit of sheep's wool, caught on the barbed wire . . . wild roses—don't think they smell . . . *fungus*. Filthy great puffball"—she forgot the gap in their ages, which normally she was quite conscious of, and felt for once, if anything, immeasurably older and more experienced than he. He might have lived longer, but there were so many things, to her so commonplace, that he had never met with.

It was strange how the very minute they reached the Kingdom, their roles were reversed: once more Abe was the one with all the experience, she the gauche sixteen-year-old anxious for approval.

"You can't light fires, of course, because of no chimney, but I have a couch—well, it's an old divan, really—and a blanket, and if you bring a hot Thermos, like we have today—"

What she would have done if he had laughed, she didn't know—certainly never brought him there again, even supposing that he'd wanted to; but being Abe, he didn't laugh. He took it quite seriously, exploring from wall to wall, learning the layout, the position of her few filched sticks of furniture, then flinging himself down on the couch, while Marianne sat cross-legged on the old car seat. He said, "This is splendid, isn't it? A real retreat. Are you sure no one's going to come and kick you out?"

"Should think they'd have done it by now if they were going to."

"Does no one ever come up here?"

"Not as far as I know. Never seen anyone."

"Some find." Abe accepted a cup of hot coffee from the Thermos and sat cradling it between his hands. "Is it—just to be on the safe side, I don't want to put my foot in it—is it one of those things that one doesn't let on about to mothers?"

"Well—I've never *purposely* kept it from her, but—"

"Best not to mention?"

"She'd only get in one of her flaps. You know what she's like: *Oh, Marianne, do you really think you ought?* and *Suppose you're trespassing?* and *What happens if you find a vagrant?* Probably try to stop me coming here."

"It means a lot to you, doesn't it," said Abe, "having this place?"

"It's somewhere where I can come to be alone. Somewhere I can *think*."

"What sort of things do you think about?"

"Oh—" Having to go to parties and not having any boyfriends and being "extraordinarily immature. . . ." "What I'll be doing five years from now and whether pigs have wings."

"What *do* you think you'll be doing five years from now?"

"Heaven knows . . . social security slacker?"

"From all I've heard of social security, that wouldn't be very much fun. You don't want to believe everything you read in the press . . . it's not all holidays in Majorca at the taxpayers' expense. Mostly it's being treated like dirt by petty bureaucrats and generally regarded as the dregs. I honestly wouldn't advise it."

"Could be I won't have much say in the matter. Way things are—who wants mediocrities?"

"Is that how you think of yourself? As a mediocrity?"

"What I mean is, I'm not particularly gifted at anything."

"Nor are the vast majority of us."

"You are," she said.

"Me?" He shook his head. "No way. I have a reasonable talent. Nothing more."

"Well, but at least you enjoy what you're doing." There was a pause. "You do," she said, "don't you?"

"Enjoy is a bit strong. I gain a certain satisfaction. Most of the time I simply thank my lucky stars that I'm capable of earning a living. There weren't an awful lot of options open to me. Certainly teaching is better than answering telephones or tuning pianos. I wouldn't say it exactly thrills me. But then, I don't think most people's jobs do. There are just a few lucky ones who have real vocations and are given the opportunity of pursuing them, but for the rest of us it's a question of getting out of it what you can and . . . looking for kicks elsewhere."

"Most people just go home and watch television."

"Sure. Well"—he grinned—"at least that's something I've been spared! A sort of consolation prize . . . can't be tempted to waste my life goggling. Tell me what you would really like to do, if you had the choice."

"If I had the choice?" She hesitated, swilling coffee to and fro in the mug from the top of the flask. "Something to do with people, I suppose."

"With people, or for people?"

"*For* people. Helping people."

"Social work? Probation officer?"

She shook her head, very firm. "Not that. I thought of that. I don't think I believe in people going to prison. I mean, I don't believe in people sitting in judgment over other people when they don't know anything about what it's really like."

"What what's really like?"

"Being tempted. Living in tower blocks and having six kids and being on welfare, and everything."

"Do *you* know what it's really like?"

"No. That's why I don't want to sit in judgment. I don't think people should."

"Hm! A bit of the old anarchist, eh? So what about medicine?"

"Not clever enough. No good at science."

"Teaching?"

She looked at him, doubtfully.

"Teaching what?"

"Whatever you're best at."

"Not best at anything."

"General, then."

She wrinkled her nose. "It's not . . . *helping* enough."

"So what do you want already? Mother Teresa? Slums of Calcutta? How about teaching in a school for the blind? *That* be helping enough?"

From somewhere in the recesses of her mind, a little tendril shot out and experimentally took hold of the idea. Teach in a school for the blind? It was not something that had ever occurred to her—it was not the sort of career that former students ever came back and talked about. Abe, sensing no doubt that he had at last found a chink in the resistance, said, "At least it's something you know you'd be good at."

Her head jerked up. "How would I know?"

"Well, you've been pretty successful at teaching me, haven't you? I make a smashing omelette now!"

As so often, she couldn't be sure whether he was serious or

teasing. "That's different," she muttered. "You're grown up."

"So kids are far easier—far more willing to go out on a limb. Not nearly so timorous and self-conscious."

"Timorous and self-conscious? You're not timorous and self-conscious!"

"You want to bet? Of course I am! Scared silly of making a fool of myself."

"You weren't scared silly of dancing."

"That was because I had you there. When I'm left to manage on my own . . . can you imagine the utter idiocy of asking a *tree* to take one across the road? Of walking into lamp posts, then standing there apologizing? I've been doing it for just about as long as I can remember, but still it makes you feel pretty dumb."

She could see that it would make *her* feel dumb—so many things did; but Abe, she had thought, took such things in his stride.

"I'm sure," he said persuasively, "that what you've done for me, you could do for kids."

For just a moment she felt excited—who could tell? Perhaps she really could.

"Would it mean teacher training?" she said.

"I imagine so. Why don't you write and find out?"

"And Braille? Would I have to learn Braille?"

"Well, at some stage."

She made a face. "All those little dots?"

"So, it's no worse than shorthand! Don't be so easily put off. If I can learn it, there's no earthly reason why you can't. Teach it to you myself, if you wanted."

She was about to leap at the opportunity with an eager:

"*Would* you?" when she remembered her mother and the eagerness subsided. She mumbled, "That'd be imposing. You know what *she* says about imposing. Be all hell to pay."

Abe made no comment, just slowly, pensively, drank his coffee. With a stab, she thought: That's it. He won't offer again.

"I suppose"—carefully he felt around for the chair without any back and set down his coffee mug—"I suppose we couldn't operate a barter system? If I were to unravel the mysteries of Braille, and you—"

She thought he was going to say, "and you bring me for walks in the country." If he were, then it wouldn't be any use. Her mother would never accept that as fair exchange. She would never believe he wasn't coming into the country just to please her.

"—and you were to read to me occasionally."

"*Read?*"

"Could you bear it? Just now and again?"

She could happily read to him all night long, if that was what he wanted. She had thought he was quite content with his big volumes full of dots.

"It's something that would be very greatly appreciated," said Abe. "It's one of the few luxuries I've forfeited that I really regret, having someone on hand to read to me."

Jealously, she said: "Did Sarah read to you?"

"When she could find the time."

"*I'll* read to you as often as you like."

"Better not make rash promises! You might find you don't care for the *Life & Work of Orlando Gibbons* or *Early Elizabethan Lute Music*—besides, we don't want your mother thinking that *I'm* imposing on *you*."

"She wouldn't."

"She would, you know, and she'd have every right—and talking of your mama, oughtn't we to be making tracks before she starts deciding that you've fed me to the cows?"

"I suppose so." Regretfully, she screwed the top back on the Thermos. Today, more than ever, she was reluctant to leave the coziness of the Kingdom, just her and Abe and nobody else, for the world and its problems that lay outside. "I sometimes wish I could stay up here forever."

"Yes, we all have dreams like that. Unfortunately, reality waits for us and there's no escaping it . . . come on! Take me back. I'm completely at your mercy—that ought to give you a sense of power."

"I don't want power," she said. "Not over other people; just over *me*."

Mrs. Fenton was watching at the window for them as they came down Star Street. Marianne, not feeling quite the same surge of irritation as she had the previous night, since at five o'clock in the evening, with both of them tired and filthy, there really wasn't very much likelihood that Abe would be going to kiss her, said simply: "There she is, peering through the curtains with her worry beads in hand. Wonder if she's rung the cop shop yet."

"You be quiet," said Abe. "You don't know when you're well off."

Mrs. Fenton, blissfully unaware—was it a property of mothers to be always so?—appeared at the door with a cheerful: "Couldn't have timed it better if you'd tried! I've just this minute turned the bath on. Who wants first soak?"

"Abe," said Marianne.

"Marianne," said Abe.

"You're the guest," said Marianne.

"Ah, but you're the lady," said Abe.

"Well, while you're fighting it out," said Mrs. Fenton, "I'll go and put the kettle on. Don't take all day, will you? Don't want the water to get cold."

11

On Monday, after English, Miss Jones beckoned Marianne to one side. "I was pleased to hear you turned up on Saturday after all," she said.

Marianne, squirming, mumbled that she had "always intended to do so."

"Yes, well, you certainly seem to have enjoyed yourself, by all accounts."

What was one supposed to say to *that?*

Miss Jones, ever helpful, said it for her: "Just make sure you keep up the good work. It can only be beneficial." She nodded, pleasantly. "After Easter I shall expect to see a definite improvement in the quality of your concentration."

"Yes," said Marianne.

Miss Jones reached the door. She turned, with what might almost have been a twinkle, except that Miss Jones wasn't much given to twinkling. "From what I'm told, your pianist friend made something of a hit. Just as well you brought him. . . . I gather the evening would have come to pretty much of a full stop if you hadn't!"

Marianne, left alone in the room, went into a mock swoon. My cup runneth over, she thought. Positively it spilleth in all directions . . .

Always in the past, even when Tip had been there, she

had looked forward to Easter break as an event most devoutly to be welcomed. For a few glorious weeks it spelled freedom, release from the tyranny of timetables and staff. Now, with only days to go before the start of it, she could without any pang of heart have postponed or even cancelled the entire period.

For the first time ever, four weeks of freedom exercised no appeal. Had Abe been going to be there, it would have been a different matter, but Abe was going to Italy and she didn't see how life was going to be any fun at all without him. Just she and her mother and nothing to do but cycle out to the Kingdom, and even that, now, would seem empty without Abe.

He himself didn't want to go away. He had told her so. He had said that he would "just as soon stay here . . . God knows I've got enough to keep me occupied, there's a hundred and one things I ought to be catching up on, and to be perfectly honest the prospect of spending four solid weeks in the company of my fond and doting mama doesn't exactly enthrall me, but—"

"So why go?" said Marianne. Abe was an adult; he could do whatever he chose. People couldn't order him about as they could her.

"I suppose," said Abe, "precisely because she *is* fond and doting."

Yes, and beastly stinking rich, thought Marianne. If she didn't have so much rotten money, she couldn't afford to go wafting him off for weeks at a time.

"Don't worry," said Abe. He ruffled her hair, consoling, big-brotherly. "I'll send you a postcard from Italy. That cheer you up?"

She wasn't in a mood to be cheered up. Abe was off first

thing tomorrow, and a whole month of emptiness stretched before her.

"Not much point," she said querulously. "Shan't be able to send you one back."

"Yes, you will! Why shouldn't you? I'll give you the address. Got a pencil and paper?"

"Yes, but what's the *use*?"

"What do you mean, what's the—oh, I see! Well, of course, if you were intending to say something *personal*—"

No doubt about it: this time he *was* teasing. What could she have to say that could ever be construed as "personal"?

"Tell you what," said Abe. "Suppose I were to give you a call? Then you could say whatever you liked. No third party . . . how about that?"

Her cheeks were already pink; now they grew even pinker.

"Cost the earth," she muttered.

"So? If I wish to call you, it's my business what it costs. You just concentrate on thinking of something nice to say!"

Abe had told her that while he was away she might play the piano just as often as she liked—"In fact, the more practice you put in, the better pleased I shall be. I shall certainly know if you've been slacking!" No danger of that. She was up there first thing every morning, the minute her mother had left for work, faithfully practicing scales and exercises for a solid hour before allowing herself the more amusing indulgence of tinkering—picking out tunes with one finger, "pretending" concertos, trying to make sense out of some of the volumes of proper music (as opposed to Braille music) Abe kept in his room. Quite often, there being not very much else to do after she had finished the dishes and the shopping and the obligatory minimum of housework, she would go back up and tinker some more or simply wander aimlessly about the room fidgeting with things, picking them up and putting them down and thinking how different it all was from when Miss Pargeter had been there. The front bedroom in Miss Pargeter's day had been full of what she used to call *objets*, every available inch of shelf and mantelshelf covered in balloon ladies and shepherdesses, straw-hatted donkeys dragging little carts, and boxes all stuck about with shells. The floor had been a veritable sea of footstools and fire-screens and long, spindly lamps that Marianne had been forever knocking over. There had been Turkish rugs and nests of occasional tables and even a brass coal scuttle, for what conceivable purpose she had never been able to imagine, since the only fire was gas, with a meter.

Abe didn't go in for knick-knackery of any kind. The floor space was spartanly clear, the shelves bare of all ornamentation, his clothes hung neatly out of sight in the wardrobe— unlike Miss Pargeter's, which had tended to hang about behind doors on ruched satin coat hangers. She knew that Abe's were hung neatly because she had collected a jacket from the cleaner's for him and had seen them when she put it away. He hadn't asked her to collect the jacket: she had caught sight of the cleaning ticket and had volunteered. It made her feel she had at least some form of contact with him while he was abroad.

It was for that very same reason that she liked to be in his room. She didn't want to pry or unlock secrets; only it comforted her to pick up the things he had left behind and touch them and feel that they were part of him, and that soon he would be coming back to use them again. In any case, she couldn't have pried even had she wanted. He had little enough there of an intimate nature. Only a few clothes, his volumes of Braille, his razor—she wondered why he hadn't taken his razor with him. She hoped it wasn't that he had forgotten to pack it. She had offered twice to help him with his packing, but he had said, "No, you do far too much for me as it is. You're not here to act as my unpaid skivvy." Now he had gone without his razor. She had known she ought to have helped him.

Time dragged as it never had before. She hadn't properly appreciated, until Abe had come to stay, how lonely she had been all those months without Tip. Of course she had been aware of the sudden void in her life, the gaping hole where once there had been companionship and confidences; but not the real, inner, deep-down aching loneliness. That was something she had always managed to conceal from herself. Books and bicycle rides and dreaming sessions in the Kingdom had safely covered it up. Books and bicycle rides still helped, to a certain extent; it was the dreaming sessions that didn't seem to work any more.

Weekends were the worst, because her mother was at home and she couldn't even solace herself by going into Abe's room and sitting down at the piano. Mrs. Fenton said she did quite enough of that during the week.

"They were telling me next door . . . nothing but Ravel's Boléro and Chopsticks from the time I go out in the morning till the time I come in again at night. I think we might at least give them a rest on Saturdays and Sundays."

"All right," said Marianne. "I won't actually play it, I'll just sit there and practice silently."

"If you want to practice silently, you can make yourself a dummy keyboard and do it on that."

"*Why?* When there's a proper piano?"

"Because you'd be tempted, that's why. We don't want to

upset people—we've all got to live together. In any case, when Abe said you could go into his room, I'm quite sure he didn't expect you to spend all day and every day mooning about in there."

She resented that: *mooning about*. Made her sound like some lovesick calf. She wished, all the same, that he would call. He had sent her a postcard of the Leaning Tower of Pisa with "Love from Abe" written on the back, and "Ms. Marianne Fenton" and the address written in another hand, presumably his mother's, and she had sent him one with a picture of the town hall flowerbeds saying: "Having a wonderful time. Wish you were here. XXX Marianne," which he might or might not understand as a joke, depending on whether his mother explained about the town hall flowerbeds or simply read out the message; but still she did wish he would call.

She sat tense every evening for a week waiting for the sound of the telephone bell, and then, when at last it came, she was out in the garden cleaning the rims of her bicycle with silver polish and didn't even hear it. It was her mother who called to her from the kitchen window. "Marianne! Telephone! Someone to speak to you."

Her heart, which had leaped up at "telephone," promptly fell again at "someone." "Someone" could only mean school— Beth Walker, in all probability, wanting to start organizing. *Now, tell me, Marianne, are you or are you not—*

"Well, come on! Don't keep him waiting! He's calling all the way from Italy."

"*Italy?*"

She was on her feet and into the house within seconds. The telephone was at the end of the hall, just by the front door, on one of Miss Pargeter's occasional tables. Breathless, she grabbed up the receiver.

"Abe?"

"Hi, there! How goes it?"

Suddenly she was struck dumb. She could think of absolutely nothing to say except "O-okay."

"I got your postcard."

"Yes, I—I got yours."

"I told you I'd call."

"Yes—" This was absurd. She was behaving like an answering machine. There must be *something* she could ask him. "Are you . . . enjoying your holiday?"

"My, my, we're very polite all of a sudden! The answer is in the affirmative, as far as it goes. Not half as much fun as being dragged backward through brambles and shoved into puddles. We're moving on to Florence tomorrow. What do you want me to send you a postcard of?"

"Oh—" She couldn't for the life of her think of a single thing that had even the remotest connection with Florence. "A—a bell tower?"

"Bell tower? Good gracious me! I'll see what can be done. By the way, my mother wants to know who's the young lady we're sending all the postcards to. I told her, it's someone who's going to say nice things to me on the telephone, maybe, if I'm lucky."

The color came flooding. Nice things? Here, on the telephone? With her mother in the kitchen and able to hear every word?

She swallowed. Perhaps he was only teasing, after all.

"Can't you think of anything nice?" he said.

"I—"

"Say anything—say the first thing that comes into your head!"

"It's—it's odd not having you here," she said.

"Is it? Well, I suppose that's quite a nice sort of thing to say—unless you simply mean that it's odd to be spared the disgusting sight of me chasing bits of food around my plate every morning."

"No! Of course I don't!" In any case, it wasn't disgusting. He couldn't help it. "I didn't mean that at *all*," she said. "I just meant that it's . . . lonely. The house. It feels empty."

"Ah! Well, that's different. That *is* quite a nice thing to say. I'll send you a kiss for that. Are you keeping up with your practicing?"

"Every day. I do a whole hour. Sometimes more. Did you know you'd forgotten to take your razor?"

"Yes. I didn't forget it, I left it behind on purpose."

"You don't mean you're growing a *beard*?" she said, in dismay.

"Why not? Don't you go for the idea? Sarah never does, either. Says it makes me look like an old rabbi. Oh, don't worry! The day before we fly back, I'll risk getting my throat cut in an Italian barber's shop and have it all shaved off again . . . just for you!"

And for Sarah, she thought.

"Do something for me in return? Could you possibly pop into the library, do you think, and get me some music?"

"Braille?" She was doubtful. "Do they—"

"No, no! Not Braille. Ordinary music. I want it for Thursdays . . . it's *John Dowland, Second Book of Songes*."

"*John Dowland*"—she pulled the telephone pad toward her—"*Second—Book—of Songs*."

"Spelled S-O-N-G-E-S—or it might be *Airs*, spelled A-Y-R-

E-S. One or the other. Do you think you could manage that for me?"

"Of course I could." Heaven knows, she had little enough else to do. "I'll go in tomorrow."

"You should be able to find a copy on the shelves. If not, perhaps you could order it? Tell them I'd be most grateful to have it by the end of the month, if at all possible."

"All right." She had already decided that if there wasn't a copy in the local library she would make a special journey to town. They were bound to have it in one of the big ones— Westminster, Holborn, somewhere like that.

"If you do get a copy, try playing one or two of them through on the piano. I think you'll like them."

She had already decided on that, as well.

"Let me know which ones particularly grab you. Might influence my final choice. Sweetheart, I must dash, I'm being yelled at to come and have dinner. See you in a bit. Until then—take care of yourself, hm?"

Marianne, in a daze, put down the receiver. He had sent her a kiss—and called her sweetheart. Of course, it didn't mean anything, she wasn't so naïve as to think that. It was only a term of endearment such as anybody might use, like down in the market where it was all "love" and "darling." Still, he wouldn't have said it if he didn't feel just a little bit fond of her, would he?

Her mother, prosaically peeling potatoes at the sink, said, "Well! All the way from Italy . . . aren't we honored!"

Marianne didn't say anything. She didn't want to ruin it. It was far too precious to be shared with her mother.

Next morning, she was down at the library even before the doors had opened. She found two volumes of Dowland on the shelves, *First Book of Songes* and *Second Book of Songes*. She took both, just to be sure. She turned the pages while she waited for the bus, skimming through the first lines. These old Elizabethans seemed dreadfully obsessed by gloom and melancholy. Everywhere you looked there were ladyes weeping, teares flowing, sorrowes staying. *There* was one that looked a bit more cheerful. "Fine knacks for ladyes, cheap choice brave and new." That was more like it. Quite jolly and bouncing. If she could only just manage to sing in tune—only manage to make a noise that was even *half*way bearable—

Well, she couldn't. She simply wasn't musical, and that was all there was to it. She didn't need Abe to tell her that she played the piano with fingers like steam hammers—she *certainly* didn't need him to tell her she had a voice like a crow. He would never be given the opportunity to find out, because she was never going to sing in front of him. He'd asked her to, on several occasions, but she wouldn't. She never did sing, save when she could be certain of being alone. Even at prayers she only mouthed, in case Miss Morgan, at the piano, should suddenly stop playing and say "Who is that girl who is droning like a bagpipe?" and everyone would know it was her, because one look at her face would be enough to tell them so.

Oh, but *why* couldn't she sing? Why *couldn't* she? She longed more than anything to be part of Abe's Thursday group. She had been consumed with pangs of wracking jealousy ever since he had told her of it. She knew that they were about her age, because they were all still at school— "couple from Rosemount, one from Hillside, a boy from the grammar—" To think that they, for three whole hours every Thursday, had the privilege of being with Abe—socially, informally, as one of themselves—and that she must be excluded only because she had a voice like a crow.

In spite of it, she spent the whole of the rest of the week going through the *Second Book of Songes*. Abe had asked her specially, because he wanted to know which ones she liked. He had even said it might influence his final choice. At least that would be something. Better than being cut out altogether. The song she liked best was "Fine Knacks for Ladyes." She sang it quite often in the bath (when her mother was out) because even her ghastly squawking voice didn't sound quite as putrid when she was there.

She was singing it thus one Friday afternoon, at the very top of her lungs, when with slow horror she became aware that someone was outside on the landing. She had heard the top step creak quite distinctly. She froze into a petrified silence. She hadn't put the chain on the front door, had she? She never did put the chain on the front door, did she? How many times had her mother told her? *Always put the chain on the front door* . . . How many times had *she*, with overconfident glibness, retorted: *Why? What is there to steal?* But it wasn't always stealing, was it? Sometimes it was rape and murder and people out of lunatic asylums . . .

Throat dry, heart hammering, she reached out for the towel. Even as she did so, a cheerful voice spoke from the other side of the door. "So what made you stop?" said Abe. "I was enjoying it . . ."

12

>>

HE HAD COME BACK A WHOLE TEN DAYS EARLY! "MY MOTHER suddenly took it into her head to go shooting off to Paris. . . . I decided the time had come to make a stand. Said I'd got things to do. After all, I am supposed to be a working man, not a lay-about. Hurry up out of that bath, I've got something for you."

She was already out of it. She had jumped out the instant she knew who it was. She hustled herself into T-shirt and jeans, braided her hair into two damp pigtails, burst out eagerly into the passage.

"Abe—*Abe!*" She stared accusingly. "You said you'd—"

"Yes! I know! Don't tell me! I apologize most abjectly—if you're referring to the beard, that is. I didn't have a chance to do anything about it. Last-minute decision, I just hopped on the first plane available and came straight back. I'd hoped," he said, "that you might be pleased to see me."

She was; of course she was! But Abe with a *beard!*

"Do you want me to remove it?"

She studied him, head to one side. It wasn't absolutely as bad as she'd thought—it was even quite distinguished, in its way. Certainly it was grossly unfair to say that it made him look like an old rabbi. On the other hand it undeniably did make him look older, and really and truly she didn't go for beards, not of any sort.

"You do want me to," said Abe. He sounded resigned. "Oh, well! Maybe next time. . . . You'd better find me some nail scissors, then you can open this."

"What is it?" she said.

"Find me some scissors, then you can open it and see."

She borrowed her mother's special manicure scissors from the top of the dressing table. She supposed if they were good enough for cutting fingernails they must be all right for cutting beards.

"Now can I open it?"

"All right. Go on."

He had bought her a bag—a beautiful Italian, real-leather bag. Not the mimsy sort with handles that mothers carried, or old ladies going to church, but a good, slinging-over-the-shoulder, three-library-books-at-a-time sort of bag. Confused, as she always was when people gave her things, she turned pink and stammered, "I d-don't know what to s-say—"

"Then don't say anything—come and give me a kiss instead. That will solve the problem."

She felt shy about kissing Abe, even though it was only thanking him for his present. Timidly she dabbed a quick peck on his cheek and retreated again to the bed. Abe said, "Well, I suppose it's better than a poke in the eye. . . . Perhaps when I've shaved this lot off I'll merit something a bit better?"

Marianne, hugging her bag, said, "Can I stay and watch?"

"Be my guest."

"I won't if you'd rather I didn't."

"Good God, what do you think I'm going to do? A striptease?—Talk to me. Keep me amused. What's been happening while I've been away?"

"Nothing. What does, in a place like this?"

"There are plenty worse. Did you get my postcard of a bell tower?"

"Yes."

"Was it a bell tower?"

"Yes."

"You amaze me! I have to rely on my mama not muddling things up. . . . She's just as likely to have sent the bell tower to Sarah and the Uffizi Gallery to you."

Of course, if she had stopped to think about it, she must have known that he would send postcards to Sarah as well as herself. When all was said and done, she was his niece.

"Did you bring Sarah something back from Italy?" she said.

"Be hideous recriminations if I didn't! I brought her a book of paintings. She's deep into art at the moment."

Well, at least that, thought Marianne, gave grounds for comfort. Art wasn't something that could very well be shared with Abe. There wouldn't be much point in taking him around an art gallery. (Why am I so hateful? she thought. Why am I always so *jealous*?)

Abe finished shaving and turned for inspection. "Better?" Shyly, she nodded. "Makes you look like you again."

"Presentable enough to have that kiss that I was never properly given?" He held out his arms. "Come on! Don't be mean . . . you know you have to treat me extra-specially nicely."

She managed it a bit better this time, but still it wasn't quite as it ought to be. Perhaps one day, she thought, he would teach her how to do it properly.

"So! Tell me"—gravely he held her at arm's length— "what's all this spiel you've been giving me about not having any voice?"

Her cheeks crimsoned. " 'Tisn't any spiel. Got a voice like a crow."

Abe raised an eyebrow; polite, disbelieving.

"Ever heard yourself?"

"Yes!"

"I don't think you have, you know. Or if you have, you've never listened properly. . . . Who told you you couldn't sing?"

"Everyone! My mother, Miss Pargeter—"

"School?"

"Never sing at school."

"You don't have any choir?"

"Didn't try for it. Knew I wouldn't get in."

She was squirming now in real embarrassment. That Abe, of all people, should have been treated to one of her appalling bathroom solos—she'd been blaring away at the top of her lungs, not caring about wrong notes, just opening her mouth and bawling.

"Come!" He swung her around, his hand very firmly beneath her elbow. She saw the piano looming up.

"Abe, no!" she said. "Please!"

"What do you mean, 'Abe, no, please!'? What's that supposed to mean?"

It means, please don't bully me into making an exhibition of myself . . . Abe, no, please!

She tried to wriggle free, but he only tightened his grip and said, "Don't be stupid, I'm far stronger than you. Where's that song you were singing? Find it!"

Dumbly, she took the *Second Book of Songes* from the top of the piano, opened it at the right page, handed it to him.

"Well, it's no good to *me*," he said, "is it?" He settled himself on the piano stool. "You look at the music, I'll pro-

vide you with an accompaniment." He played a few preliminary chords, gave her the introductory bars.

Her throat tightened. "Abe, I c—"

"You just shut up and do as you're told! Right? Right."

It sounded terrible. She knew that it did. Her voice broke
on all the top notes, she sang alternately flat and sharp and by
the end was almost weeping with the shame of it. To be
forced, in front of Abe . . .

"I told you," she said. "I *told* you!"

Abe, seemingly unmoved, took out his handkerchief, said,
"Blow your nose. Let's take it again—this time, I think, a
different key. . . . Try this."

She was horrified. "I can't sing down there!"

"Think high," said Abe, "sing low. Stop being self-
conscious. Concentrate on the words."

"But I—"

"*Marianne!*" For just a second he sounded almost angry.
"Will you kindly allow me to know what I'm talking about? I
may not be much use on a pair of skis, and maybe I can't go
for walks in the country without someone to guide me, but I
do know a potential voice when I hear one! You think I'm
some kind of sadist? Putting you through agonies just for the
hell of it? Pull yourself together and don't be such a drip! I
didn't break down in floods of tears when you insisted on frog-
marching me through the woods, did I? No, I didn't! I suffered in silence and afterward discovered that it wasn't nearly
as bad as I'd thought. . . . So! What I can do, you can do. Try
it again."

This was a side of Abe she had never seen. She had only
ever known him good-natured, self-mocking, easy-going. She
wasn't sure that she liked this new version. In a gentler voice,

as if guessing, he said, "Trust me . . . I wouldn't ask you to do anything I didn't think you were capable of."

Four times in all he made her sing it. By the fourth time, even she was starting to hear the difference—not so much hear it, perhaps, as feel it, inside herself. One minute she knew that she was indisputably, diabolically awful; the next—

"It wasn't actually g-*good*," she said cautiously.

"But a damn sight better than it was! Give it a chance—you've only just discovered it. No wonder you were so certain you couldn't sing, screeching away in a soprano register. . . . You're not a soprano, you're an alto! I thought you probably were. I just couldn't see how I was ever going to get you to the point of actually opening your mouth and demonstrating the fact—but I knew you had to have a voice of some kind. I could tell from listening to your speaking voice. Unless you'd been *absolutely* unmusical, which you certainly are not—even though you do play the piano like an elephant in boxing gloves."

She accepted the charge meekly enough; she knew it to be true. Somehow it didn't seem so important any more.

"Abe," she said breathlessly, "can I really sing?"

"Shall I crush your pretensions and say that at this precise moment the answer is no?"

She was crestfallen. "Oh—"

"But that given a bit of time and effort it may well become yes? Basically what you need is confidence. You lack technique, of course, but that's something that can soon be remedied—if you would like it to be remedied, that is?"

If she would like it? *If?* She longed to be able to ask him, *Will I ever be good enough to join the Thursday group?* but she didn't dare. Instead, humbly, in case it should be classed as pretension and need crushing, she said, "We couldn't—couldn't work at it—instead of—piano—could we?"

"Might just be able to," said Abe. He ran his fingers over the keys. "Do it once more for me?"

This time she was very willing. Already it felt more natural *not* to be "screeching away in a soprano register"; already she could hear that her voice was filling out and steadying, no more wobbles and cracks, though sometimes there was a rather unpleasant slurping effect like drinking soup as she moved from low notes (which now seemed very low indeed) to high. Abe said that was because the low notes were chest notes and the high notes came from her head, and that it was "simply a question of learning how to bridge the gap. In the old days, they didn't bother. Just went up and down like seesaws. Ever heard of a lady called Clara Butt? Makes you feel quite queasy just listening to her! Nowadays we're more sophisticated. We've evolved better ways of doing it."

"So how—"

"Just a matter of technique. I'll show you."

She wished that he would show her right now. She would have liked to go on singing all night, but it was almost four o'clock and her mother would be in at five, expecting tea to be ready and waiting, and Abe needed to go to the supermarket to do some shopping.

"In any case, that's quite enough for now. We can always give it a go again tomorrow."

"Morning?" she said eagerly.

"Whichever suits you. My time is my own."

"So's mine," said Marianne.

"All right, then. Let's strike a bargain. . . . I'll give you singing lessons in the morning, you take me out for walks in the afternoon. That do you?"

It was hard to think of anything that could possibly do her better; but yet there was something. On the way back from the supermarket, with Marianne prattling nineteen to the dozen about nothing of the least importance and remembering every few seconds, in the nick of time, that Abe was with her and she couldn't go skipping on and off curbs and dodging around lamp posts the way she usually did, he quite suddenly interrupted her with: "Tell me—if you can stop talking just for one second—now that I've managed to convince you that you do have some kind of a voice: How would you feel about joining us on Thursdays?"

She stopped dead in her tracks.

"On Th-*Thurs*days? To s-*sing*?"

"Well, we don't dance hornpipes. . . . Do you mind concentrating on what you're supposed to be doing, by the way? Life's quite perilous enough without you coming to sudden screeching halts when I'm least expecting it. Yes, of course to sing! We're badly in need of a decent alto. How about it? Would you care to?"

The beam that spread across her face was so ecstatic that it impeded speech. She tried to open her mouth and say something, but all that came out was a series of small squeaks as the laughter bubbled up. It was the sort of idiot laughter that proceeds from a bliss almost too great to be borne.

"Well?" said Abe. "What is that supposed to be taken as meaning? Yes—or no?"

"*Yes!*" she said. "Please!"

13

THE THURSDAY GROUP MET IN THE HOME OF ONE OF THE girls from Rosemount. Predictably, she lived over on the far side of town, in what Marianne privately thought of as "the posh part."

"Have they got a butler?" she asked.

"Good God, I shouldn't imagine so!" Abe seemed amused. "If they have, they keep him discreetly hidden . . . I've certainly never seen one."

It was odd, she thought, the way Abe always referred to "seeing" things—yet upon reflection what else was he to say? I've never heard one? Never bumped into one? Perhaps that would seem even odder.

"Are they going to resent me?" she said.

"Of course they're not going to resent you! Why on earth should they? You do have the strangest ideas about your fellow human beings."

"It's just that . . . outsiders aren't always welcome, are they?"

"You're not an outsider." Firmly, he tucked her arm through his. "You belong with me and no one will dream of resenting you. Turn left at the end of this road, by the way. It's the first house on the right."

The first house on the right was enormous and detached, with a great horseshoe drive and double garage, and a plastic canopy shaped like a shell over the front door.

"Nouveau Georgiana," hissed Marianne.

"Really?" said Abe. "Nobody ever told me."

The door was opened not by a butler or even an au pair, but by the girl from Rosemount with the face of a Madonna.

She took one look at Marianne and shrieked: "Abe! Is it our alto?"

"You've got it," said Abe. "Marianne, this is Hilary . . . Hilary, Marianne."

"Glory be!" Hilary held out a hand. "Are we pleased to see *you!*" Marianne began to feel slightly alarmed. "Abe's been promising us for weeks. He said he thought he'd found someone, but he couldn't be quite sure—didn't you once come up to Rosemount to meet him? I seem to remember seeing you. You had on a green uniform; Combe House?"

"Yes," said Marianne. (She thought: *There is no need for jealousy. . . .*)

"Well, come on up. The others are all here. Come and be introduced."

They followed her up a flight of broad, red-carpeted stairs into a room that could only be her own private sitting room. It had posters on the wall, a small piano, a portable television, shelves full of books, a cabinet for records. A boy, with his back turned, was bending over the record player. Another boy and a girl with very short, bubbly red hair were at the piano studying some music. Hilary, striking a pose in the doorway, said, "Ta-ra, ta-ra! Ladies and gentlemen . . . the relief of Lucknow! Our alto has arrived!" Abe, feeling for

Marianne's hand, murmured, "Told you you'd be welcome."
Marianne only felt more alarmed than ever. He hadn't told
her they were actually *relying* on her.

The boy at the piano was introduced as "Graham . . . one
of our basses, Abe being the other, but you probably know
that already." The girl with the red hair was Ginny—"only a
soprano, I'm afraid we're two a penny. Can't get a decent
alto for love or money." (Marianne's hand, still clasped in
Abe's, shook slightly.)

"And this," said Hilary, "is Stephen, our one and only
tenor—even more difficult to come by than altos."

The boy bending over the record player straightened up
and turned into Stephen Derwent. She recognized him at
once. He, quite obviously, recognized her. For just a second
they stood looking at each other.

Snob school, innit?

*Well, at any rate it's better than where you're going . . .
anyone can go to Hillside. You don't even have to* PAY *to go*
THERE . . .

Marianne said, "Hallo."

Stephen seemed to weigh matters within himself and come
to a decision. Abruptly he stuck out his hand. "Hi, alto.
How's Star Street?"

"Okay. How's—" She couldn't think of the name of the
estate where he lived. "How's Hillside?"

He grinned. "Same as ever—you still don't have to pay to
go there."

"For God's sake! Don't get her started on that," said Abe.
"She's got this great hate thing about private education."

Marianne turned pink. Stephen shot her a curious glance.

"Do I take it," said Hilary, "that you two already know
each other?"

"Oh, we go way back," said Stephen. "Way, way back. . . . Remember how we used to sit on the building site shoveling sand into each other's navels?"

Abe said, "For crying out loud!" Stephen looked at Marianne and winked; she knew then that it was going to be all right.

The songs they sang that first evening were all from the *Second Book* by John Dowland. Thanks to Abe, she was already familiar with them. She found she could keep her line quite well, even when other voices all around her were coming in at different places and setting up in competition. She did rather wish that Miss Jones might see her. *What clubs do you belong to? What group things do you do? How are you going to cope with work if you don't like doing things with people?* But she had said at the time—hadn't she?—I don't mind *doing* things. It was the not doing things that had always bothered her. Just being in a big aimless heap doing nothing. That was what she wasn't good at—or hadn't been, until this evening. This evening, when they had had enough singing, they all flopped down on the floor, scattering themselves about on rugs and cushions, while Ginny, with the bright-red bubbly hair, went along to the bathroom with the electric kettle and made instant coffee from a jar that was kept on the mantelshelf, along with a box of powdered milk and a box of sugar. Marianne, feeling that as a newcomer she ought to be ingratiating herself, said, "Can I help?" but Stephen promptly pulled her down again.

"We've got a rota—take it strictly in turns. Don't you worry, we'll have you on it before you know where you are. No one gets out of it except Abe."

"Who is excused," said Abe, "on the grounds of being generally above that sort of thing."

"Who is excused," retorted Stephen, "on the grounds of being generally incompetent!"

Abe smiled lazily. "Actually, I'm not any more, thanks to Marianne—but I don't mind going on being excused. It's only right you young people should wait on your elders and betters."

"Granddad!" said Graham.

Hilary, producing a packet of custard creams (it seemed they had a dessert rota as well, from which Abe was *not* excused) said, "Now that we've got a proper alto we can start planning things. You are going to keep coming, aren't you, Marianne?"

"She'd better," said Abe, "after all the trouble I went to to discover her. Talk about a shrinking violet!"

"I thought these posh fee-paying schools were supposed to bolster your ego," said Stephen.

"Not Marianne's. She genuinely thought she had a voice like a crow. I had to threaten her with violence. Wasn't till she opened her mouth to scream that we started getting anywhere. *N'est-ce pas?*" He leaned across to nudge Marianne. "*Vrai ou non?*"

"You bullied me," she said.

From across the room Ginny sang out, "When doesn't he? You ought to see him at school . . . comes into class with a horsewhip!"

The banter went on—and she was part of it. She sat there, on the floor, cross-legged next to Abe, on a big, fat, foam-filled cushion, eating custard creams and drinking coffee out of a cracked mug, and no one thought she was odd or peculiar or an isolationist. Already she was one of them, to be placed on the coffee list and the dessert rota and included in their plans for the future. There was much excited talk about a charity concert, to be given later in the year, in which they had been asked to participate—"Can we do 'The Silver Swan,' Abe? *Please*, Abe! Now that we've got Marianne . . . say that we can!"—and a great deal of earnest discussion as to whether or not it would be right to accept an invitation from the local vicar (Hilary's) to take part in the Christmas carol concert in aid of Save the Children.

"It is in a good cause," said Stephen.

"Oh, I'm not bothered about the *cause*," said Hilary.

"What, then?"

"Well . . . it's religious, isn't it?"

"So?"

"So I'm not sure that it's right—when people aren't."

"Which people aren't? You are."

"Yes, but you're not."

Marianne felt bold enough to say: "Neither am I. I don't believe in religion."

"Well, that's it," said Hilary, sounding worried.

"It isn't it at all," said Stephen. "What's it matter what people *are*? Just because one doesn't believe in religion, that doesn't stop one believing in children."

"But what about Abe?"

"Oh, he believes in children too," said Abe.

"Yes, but are you *allowed* to?"

"Believe in children?"

"Sing carols—in church."

"Anyone's allowed to," said Stephen. "Don't be so parochial, or whatever the word is."

"I'm not being. I was thinking of Abe."

"Maybe I could get a special dispensation from the Pope?"

"Oh, do be *serious*," begged Hilary. She seemed rather a serious sort of girl. "It's no laughing matter. We've got to decide."

"Why don't you have a look around," said Abe, "and see what interesting carols you can find. Then we can take it from there. I don't imagine anyone wants 'Away in a Manger' or 'Good King Wotsisname'?"

"I wouldn't mind 'In Dulci Jubilo,'" said Hilary.

"Well, see what you can come up with. We could always give it a new arrangement. Now, what about this summer music school? Last two weeks in August." (Marianne pricked up her ears.) "What's the verdict?"

Hilary said, "Yes. Definitely—and they've said I can have the car, so that's transport enough for five, provided no one objects to a bit of a crush."

Five. Abe, Stephen, Hilary, Ginny, Graham—and Marianne. Well, she thought, trying to be brave, she couldn't expect everything at once. She'd only just joined them. She couldn't expect them to squeeze in six where there was only room for five.

Abe said, "Okay. Fine. I'll send off for details. Now—" He scrambled to his feet. "Where's Marianne? Time we were making a move before your mama starts thinking I've spirited you off somewhere."

Ginny, with a groan, said, "God, is she like mine? *When I was your age I had to be in by nine o'clock sharp* . . ."

"Marianne's mother is all right," said Abe. "It's just that she doesn't regard me as a particularly suitable escort—and who should blame her?" Marianne looked up at him, frowning. What did he mean by that? Of course her mother regarded him as suitable—*she* was only worried about imposing. Abe, as if sensing her gaze upon him, said lightly, "Well, let's face it, I wouldn't be much use to you if we were set on by a horde of muggers, would I?"

"Muggers!" said Marianne.

"Mine's got this phobia about dope," said Ginny. "Thinks everyone I meet's going to be sky high on pot and crazed to the eyeballs with LSD. She's only letting me go in August because Abe's going to be there and she reckons that makes it respectable."

"Poor trusting fool," said Stephen.

It wasn't until they were on the bus, on the way home, that Abe said, "How about it, then? Fancy a couple of weeks down in Devon?"

Her heart almost stopped.

"*Me?*" she said. "But . . . there are only five places. In the car."

"Oh, you don't have to let that worry you. We can always work something out—you and I could go down by train, if necessary. Or maybe Stephen might go on his bike; I believe he was talking of it originally. How would your mother feel, do you think? Would she be likely to agree?"

She's got to, thought Marianne. She wasn't missing out on a chance like this.

"If you're troubled about the cost, by the way, I can put your mind at rest. I'm not sure exactly what they charge, but I do know it's something purely nominal if you're still a student."

"And if we told her it was educational—"

"Which it is."

"Which it *is*."

"Who would it be better coming from? You or me?"

"You," said Marianne.

"You reckon?"

"Positive. You set the seal of respectability."

"Hm." Abe smiled. "I think perhaps I'd better stress that four other people are coming as well. . . . Sets an even stronger seal."

14

>>>

THE SUMMER SEMESTER LOOKED SET TO BE ABOUT AS
different from the previous one as could well be imagined.
On the very first day back, she arrived to find that Mary-Jane
had saved her a seat—Meg on one side of her, Marianne on
the other. Her name was down for a rounders match against
Rosemount, Beth Walker was organizing an end-of-semester
walk in aid of the local handicapped and was relying on
Marianne to help plan the route, "because someone said
you're good at walking," Jo Dyer from the junior class
wanted to know whether "you and your boyfriend" would be
interested in coming to a new disco that was opening in the
High Street next month. Marianne said cautiously that she
would inquire. She couldn't imagine that the opening of a
new disco would hold very much appeal for Abe, but the
mere fact that she had been asked—that she was thought to
be the possessor of a bona fide boyfriend—was enough to
carry her along on a crest of euphoria.

Not only that; Abe wasn't going home at weekends any
more. He said it was ridiculous, at his age, to be running back
to his married sister every five days just to get a square meal
and his laundry done.

"I shall go out and buy fish and chips and learn how to use
the launderette the same as everyone else."

"I'll show you," said Marianne.

"Just the once, then," said Abe. "After that I do it for myself. Right?"

She said, "Right," but she didn't see why, on weeks when they both had to go, they shouldn't do it together. He could put his own things in the machine and measure out his own soap powder and set his own switches if that was what he wanted. She wouldn't interfere.

She asked him, the first time, as they sat watching the washing go around—as she sat watching the washing go around, and Abe sat patiently waiting—if he had ever been to a disco. He said, "Only once. Nearly blew my eardrums out. Why? Do you fancy the idea?"

Do I *always* have to be so transparent? she thought. Can I *never* ask him a simple question without him instantly knowing why I have asked it?

"Oh, not really," she said. She leaned forward to make some totally unnecessary adjustment to the setting of the machine. "It's just that some girl at school wanted to know if we"—hastily, she corrected herself—"*I* felt like going to one next Saturday. There's a new one opening in the High Street. She thinks it should be quite good. I don't expect it will be. Nothing but noise and cigarette smoke. They say if the decibels are too high you can actually get deaf from it."

"I'm prepared to believe it," said Abe. He was silent a moment, then: "You ever been to one?"

She made a face. "No. I was going once with Tip" (she had told him about Tip—she had told him about most things by now) "but they wouldn't let us. Seemed to think we were going to be kidnapped by white slave traders and hauled off to the nearest brothel."

The ghost of a smile flickered across Abe's face. "Well, I can't imagine anyone wanting to kidnap *me* and haul me off to the nearest brothel. Suppose we chained our wrists together and left the key at home? Then it would have to be both of us or neither."

"But—do you really *want* to?"

"I'll strike one of our bargains," said Abe. "I'll come with you to this disco, if the Saturday after you'll come with me to a concert . . . it's an old college friend of mine. He's giving a Mozart recital at some way-out place over in north London. He's sent me a couple of comps, but I haven't the faintest, remotest idea of how I'm supposed to get there. So if you're prepared to take me to my Mozart, I'll take you to your disco. Fair exchange?"

It was more than fair; she actually quite liked Mozart.

Saturday evening they went to the disco, with Jo Dyer and a crowd of others, and it was all very psychedelic and a new experience, but the place was jam-packed and the sort of dancing that people did wasn't the sort that Abe could join in, and more than that she kept worrying about the level of the decibels and whether it might be high enough to do harm to one's hearing. For herself she wasn't bothered; it was for Abe. Not to be able to see *and* to have his eardrums damaged—and all her fault for dragging him there when she had known that it wasn't really his scene.

They stayed for just over an hour, then Marianne said urgently, "Abe, let's go!"

"Why? Have you had enough?" he asked.

"Yes!"

"Are you sure? It's not just because of me?"

"No! I want to go—*now!*"

"Come on, then," said Abe. "Get me out of this seething throng and I'll stand you a coffee somewhere very, very quiet where we don't have to shout."

It really was much better, just being with Abe by himself than in a disco full of people. She had never been one for a crowd.

On Thursday, when they broke for coffee, Graham came and sat down beside her and after a bit of preliminary throat clearing said, "I suppose you wouldn't care to come to a party with me on Saturday, by any chance, would you?" She was surprised that he should ask her. Not just that he should ask her, but that he should actually do so in front of Abe. She had always thought that the Thursday group accepted that she and Abe belonged together. Whenever they finished singing for the evening and spread themselves about on the floor to be cozy and talk, someone always saved her a cushion next to him even when it was her turn to make the coffee and she was the last to sit down. Likewise, when they went back up the road at the end of the evening, it was taken for granted that Marianne was the one who was going to walk with Abe, not Stephen or Graham or Ginny.

Six months ago an invitation to a party would have thrown her into a nervous fluster of agitation. Now, politely, but with just the tiniest of frowns to indicate that she wasn't free to go to parties—or at any rate, not with other men—she said, "It's very nice of you, and I'd love to, but as it happens I'm going to a concert with Abe."

Graham said, "Oh—oh, I see" and a slow tide of scarlet began washing over his face. It was a pleasant enough face—round and slightly chubby, with smooth pink cheeks and a dimpled chin—and Graham was a pleasant enough boy; she felt sorry that she had made him blush, because she knew how devastating it was, but really he should have known better. To her horror, just as she was on the point of explaining about its being Mozart and way over in north London and one of Abe's friends from college, Abe himself broke in with: "Why don't you go? You needn't feel duty bound to play escort to me—they were free tickets, anyway. Not as if I paid for them."

"No!" She was indignant. "We struck a bargain!"

"Well, I don't mind releasing you from it. I shan't hold it against you. Even I know that a party is far more fun than a Mozart recital."

Graham, perhaps, was brighter than his round, chubby face would seem to indicate. Taking one look at Marianne, he blushed even deeper than ever but managed to mumble that it was all right, it wasn't going to be a particularly good party in any case, and he had only asked on the off chance. He then jumped up to help Stephen bring the coffee over, which showed, thought Marianne, rare tact.

Rare tact was more than Abe could be said to show. He didn't mention anything on the bus, because Stephen was with them, but almost before they were out of earshot he returned to the attack with: "Why didn't you say yes to Graham when I gave you the opportunity? He's a shy lad. He's probably been bolstering up his courage for the past four weeks to ask you to go somewhere with him."

"But I don't want to go anywhere with him! I'm not a charity institution."

"Some people might say that you were. You're prepared to trek halfway across London only for the sake of taking me to a recital that will almost certainly bore you silly—"

"It will not bore me silly!" She resented that almost more than anything. "I like Mozart!"

"But if you went to a party you would meet people. It would be far better for you."

Better for her! He was sounding like Miss Jones—and why would it be better for her? Mozart was culture, wasn't he?

Answering her unspoken question, Abe said, "You ought to be going out with someone your own age—someone who can take you to discos and go dancing and drive you down to Brighton and—oh, all the things that I can't do. You shouldn't be lumbering yourself with someone like me."

"What do you mean, *someone like you*?"

"You know very well what I mean . . . I wish you'd call Graham up and say you'd changed your mind. I'd feel far happier."

Without warning, tears sprang to her eyes. "You're not being fair! We made a bargain! How would you get there if I didn't come with you?"

"Oh, I could find a way if I really had to. I could always give Sarah a ring, or get someone to put me in a cab at Victoria. . . . I'm just taking advantage of you, you see. *That's* how I'm not being fair. If playing nursemaid to me is going to stop you going to parties with Graham—"

"I don't want to go to parties with Graham!"

"Marianne, you're young," said Abe. "You ought to be getting out and enjoying yourself—like Hilary and Steve. They play tennis, they go to the movies, sometime soon they're going off on some rock-climbing expedition. That's the sort of thing you ought to be doing. Not acting as my unpaid guide dog."

The tears now were coming in earnest, rolling down her cheeks and dripping off the end of her nose. She needed desperately to take out her handkerchief, but didn't dare for fear of alerting Abe. She held her head back, trying to stem the flow, scarcely able to see where she was going for the blur before her eyes.

"Marianne?" Abe stopped. She, perforce, stopped with him. They were on the corner of Star Street, at the junction of the Brown Bear and the National Westminster Bank. The High Street, behind them, was still full of activity, traffic roaring, movie theaters disgorging, snack bars neon-lighted. Star Street, ahead, lay silent and deserted, waiting for closing time and the Brown Bear to empty. "Have I made you cry?" said Abe.

She tried to say no, because she was ashamed of crying, even in front of Abe—perhaps especially in front of Abe— but all that came out was a ruptured squawk. She groped like a mole for her handkerchief.

"I have," said Abe, "haven't I?" He put up a hand and felt her face, awash in a sea of salt. He sounded as if it bothered him, that he had made her cry. It hadn't bothered him before, when he had bullied her into singing for him. Then he had simply thrust a handkerchief at her and told her not to be such a drip. Now, as she located her own handkerchief and blew vigorously at her nose with it, he said, "I didn't mean to. I was only thinking of you."

She hiccuped, angrily. "I w-wish people w-*wouldn't*. I'm not a ch-*child*. I can th-think quite w-well for mys-*self*."

"I'm sure you can," said Abe.

"Well, I c-can! And don't"—she hiccuped again, more violently than before—"say horrid th-things."

"I didn't say horrid things, sweetheart, I—"

"Yes, you did! About not acting as an unpaid g-guide dog!"

"That wasn't horrid, it—"

"It was horrid! It was h-hateful!"

He was obviously puzzled. Gently he said: "How was it hateful?"

"It just w-*was*."

"It wasn't intended. I promise you. I was only th—" He stopped. "I mustn't say that, must I?"

"No! I'm sick to *death* of people *only thinking of me*. Why can't they try thinking of themselves for a change and leave me to th-think for mys-self?"

"Don't be angry."

"Then stop t-treating me l-like a ch-child!" Even as she said it, she was aware that she was behaving like one. Her voice broke, self-pitying. "I suppose that's all you th-think of me . . . just a ch-child."

"It isn't all I think of you."

"Sometimes s-seems like it."

"Well, it isn't. You want me to prove it?"

She sniffed. "Bit l-late now. Trying to make me go to p-parties with other p-people—"

She was behaving not only like a child, but like a silly, spoiled, ungracious child. Abe, however, only said, "Marianne . . . come here."

"W-what for?"

She stood defiantly, facing him across the pavement. Had he said: "Do as you're told," even jokingly, she wouldn't have gone. Instead he said, "Please?" and so she did.

"Wh-what do you—"

"Hush!" said Abe.

There, at the corner of Star Street, at the junction of the Brown Bear and the National Westminster, he put his arms about her. There, on the corner of Star Street, at half-past ten on a Thursday night, with activity going on all around them, he kissed her. Not just a peck on the cheek, but properly. She knew that it was properly. Even though it had never happened before, she knew. They had been warned about letting themselves be kissed like that—"in a certain way" was how Dr. Hargreaves had put it, in her famous now-we-are-growing-up-and-must-be-told-the-facts-of-life lecture at the end of the fourth year, only no one ever took the slightest bit of notice of anything Dr. Hargreaves said. She wore hand-knitted cardigans that wrapped around her twice over and was long past the age of being kissed in any way at all.

"Never let your boyfriends make free with you." That was one of the things she said. "Never let them Go Too Far . . . you will only forfeit their respect, and it will inevitably lead to Unfortunate Consequences."

She hadn't specified what the unfortunate consequences were, but everyone had known, even in the fourth. Some people, like Mary-Jane, had sniggered. Others, like Marianne, had grown red and started coughing. Not that she had imagined anyone would ever want to make free with her, being so immature and looking like a carthorse to boot.

"There," said Abe. "That's what you get when I stop thinking of *you* and start thinking only of myself."

She wondered if she had forfeited his respect (if he had ever had any in the first place). Would he now despise her utterly? Perhaps she ought to have stopped him. Said something like: "Please don't" or—very icy, very controlled— "Kindly unhand me . . ."

She giggled.

"What's so funny?" said Abe.

"I was wondering if I should have said: 'Kindly unhand me'—"

"You'd have had a nerve! After telling me to stop treating you like a child? You can't have it both ways."

"I don't want it both ways." Just the one way. The way that it had just been. "Abe—" She took his hand. "Can I come with you to the Mozart? *Please?*"

"I suppose you'll have to," said Abe. "Never let it be said that I missed an opportunity to instill a bit of culture . . ."

15

>>>

LIFE, ALL OF A SUDDEN, WAS MORE FULL THAN IT HAD EVER
been, even in the days of Tip—and how remote those days
seemed now. Writing to Tip had become almost like writing
to a stranger. All the old jokes had been outgrown, the secrets once shared lost their savor. She and Tip were two
quite different people. She had the feeling that if they were
to meet they would have nothing any more in common. Tip
wrote of her sheep shearer and of going to dances, of secre-
tarial college and shorthand tests at 100 words per minute;
Marianne wrote of school and the Thursday group, of Abe
and teacher training. Soon, very soon, the correspondence
would dwindle to birthday cards and Christmas, to Christmas
cards and nothing. A few months ago she would have been
bereft; today she was almost too busy even to notice the
loss.

There was no more talk of her going to parties with other
people. If she went to parties with anyone, it was with Abe,
but mostly, apart from the Thursday group, they preferred
doing things on their own. On Mrs. Fenton's bridge nights
they still cooked a meal together and ate it upstairs in Abe's
room. Afterward they would listen to music, or do some
work on a song, or else Marianne would read aloud or Abe
might play the piano. They were never short of things to

keep them occupied. If they tired of music or reading there was always the crossword or Scrabble, on a special Scrabble set that had the tiles printed in Braille as well as in ordinary letters. Abe said that next time he went home he would bring back his chess set and teach her how to play chess, but in the meantime Scrabble did them very well.

Every Thursday there were meetings of the group, and now, with the beginning of September and the charity concert only just over two months away ("It may sound a lot," said Abe, "but it isn't") and with vacation going to intervene, they were getting together on Saturday afternoons as well. Afterward, sometimes, the others would go off and play tennis, or go to the movies or to a party, and just occasionally Abe would worry that she wasn't going with them and would say that he didn't mind if she wanted to, but always she managed to convince him that she didn't—because it was true, she didn't; not without him. She and Abe would usually go off by themselves to a concert, or maybe catch the bus and go out to the Kingdom, for now the evenings were lengthening and it was light until almost ten o'clock, and not even her mother could worry about muggers or dope fiends in the depths of the country.

In the middle of June there was a heat wave and everyone ran around in shirt sleeves and skimpy blouses, sweating profusely and in tones of rather desperate conviction saying how lovely it was, wasn't it? In Hilary's garden there was a pool, and now on Thursdays, and Saturdays as well, instead of sitting around drinking coffee they would tear off their clothes—their swimsuits were already on—and go swarming outside to leap in the water. At first Abe wouldn't join them; he said he would be quite happy just sitting on the side listening to them and dabbling the occasional foot.

Marianne wondered for a moment if perhaps she too ought to go and sit on the side and dabble a foot, because it didn't seem fair, her enjoying herself and Abe not, but then Stephen said, "Race you three lengths!" and plunged in and she couldn't resist the challenge of plunging in after him. When he had won and she had come second and the others nowhere at all, they all joined forces in an attempt to coax Abe.

"Come on, Granddad! Don't know what you're missing!"

"Yes, come on, Abe! We won't let you drown!"

"What's the matter? Can't he swim?"

"He can swim," said Abe. "When he wants to."

"Well, come on in, then!"

It was Stephen, in the end, who persuaded him—if persuaded was the word. Catching him by the ankles, he said, "Are you coming voluntarily, or do I have to pull?" Before Marianne could shriek: "Stephen! Don't!" he had pulled.

"*Stephen!*" she exclaimed.

"It's all right, it's all right, don't panic. I'm not going to let anything happen to him."

"You just wait," gasped Abe, breaking surface.

Stephen grinned. "Yes, sir—hundred lines, sir? Come on! Grab hold! Give you a guided tour."

Stephen and Marianne were the two best swimmers. While the others paddled and splashed, they had races—"one length breast stroke, one backstroke, one free style . . . go!"— and took running dives off the edge of the pool. Stephen wasn't at all like the skinny guttersnipe in short trousers and ragged jersey that she remembered from the days of their infancy. He had grown tall and broad-shouldered, with a chest like a heavyweight boxer's and thick, copper-colored hair almost down to his shoulders. He was, quite definitely, what most people would call handsome; not just attractive, but handsome. Graham wasn't in the least what people would call handsome. He was a little bit tubby and rather soft and pink, but he was cuddly, like a woolly toy. Abe was what people called nice looking—until he turned around and they saw that he couldn't see, when if they were stupid they were put off, and if they weren't they thought "Oh dear, what a shame." She knew that was what they thought, because she had seen them thinking it. The thing was that once you had gotten used to it, it didn't really make any difference; it was only just at first that it bothered you. Now that she knew him so well she had almost stopped noticing. Abe was Abe and that was how he was. Even when she was running and diving with Stephen, she never wished that she might belong to him instead of Abe. In any case, Stephen belonged to Hilary. In the autumn they were both going to be students in London, Hilary at the university studying English, Stephen at Guy's studying medicine. He wanted to become a surgeon. She often wondered, a little maliciously, what her mother would make of it: a boy from Hillside doing as well as a girl from Rosemount. It just went to show—it was what she had always said. There simply wasn't any point in paying out good money for How Now Brown Cow and the Duchess of Somewhere at Speech Day.

Hilary asked her one day what she was going to do when she left school. She told her, but hesitantly, because doubts even now sometimes crept in. Was she really and truly certain? And if she was—*could* she?

"Oh, but you must!" said Hilary. "You're so good with Abe—honestly, he's doing things now that he would never have done before." (It always gave her a jolt to remember that Hilary and Ginny had known Abe for almost a year longer than she had.) "We'd never in a month of Sundays have gotten him to come swimming with us."

"Well, but that was Stephen," said Marianne, "not me."

"It might have been Stephen *immediately*, but it was you *basically*. Six months ago Steve wouldn't have pulled him into the water like that—not because he'd have gotten mad at him, because Abe never does, but just that it wasn't the sort of thing that one did. We were all too busy treating him like porcelain: 'Come and sit down, Abe,' and 'Here's a chair, Abe,' and 'Can you manage all right, Abe?' Like with the coffee rota—he *could* have made coffee, if we hadn't excused him."

"It's better to let him do things for himself," said Marianne, "even if it does take him longer."

"Well of course it is, but you see we never did. Not until you arrived. Perhaps we *ought* to start making him make coffee?"

"He'll break hundreds of cups," said Marianne.

"So who minds about cups? It's all in a good cause."

On Primrose Adcock Day (in memory of Primrose Adcock, who had been an early Combe House girl, and a suffragette, and chained herself to railings) Beth Walker had organized an outing to the British Museum. She said that it was "disgraceful . . . it's right there on our own doorstep and we never so much as look at it." Someone had said, "Speak for yourself! I practically live there." Most people had agreed, vaguely, that it *was* disgraceful and they never *did* so much as look at it and yes, they really *ought* to go. Mary-Jane, who had developed a tendency this semester to become rather matey-matey, on account of herself and Marianne being, as she confidingly put it, "the only two to have proper *men*," had dug Marianne in the ribs and whispered, "Might as well . . . we can always lose ourselves." Marianne was by no means certain that she wanted to lose herself, at any rate not with Mary-Jane, but since Miss Jones would approve, and it was undoubtedly more pleasant to be in Miss Jones's good books than her bad, she had said that she would go and authorized the writing of her name in large felt-tip letters on the list.

When the time came she wished that she hadn't, because the weather was scorching and far more conducive to lying about in the back garden doing nothing than trailing up to London to visit museums, but her mother said firmly, "You can't let people down. They're relying on you," which she had thought was ridiculous until she arrived at the station to find that only Beth and Mary-Jane and a couple of others had turned up.

"There!" said Beth. "I *said* Marianne would come."

Her tone implied: she might not do things very often, but when she says that she will then she does. Let virtue be its own reward, thought Marianne. It certainly didn't seem as if much else was going to be. No one had taken the trouble to find out exactly what was in the British Museum other than Egyptian mummies (according to Beth) and Elgin Marbles (Emily Rivers-Smith). Mary-Jane said, "Marbles as in *lost his marbles*? Or marbles as in game?"

Emily said, "Don't be so stupid, it's a *frieze*."

"As in refrigerator," murmured Marianne.

Glibness didn't pay; from that point on, Mary-Jane stuck with her doggedly. She had evidently decided that she and Marianne were two of a kind and viewed things in the same light. Marianne, tramping with glum interest around the

Egyptian room, found Mary-Jane forever at her elbow proffering hoarse titbits of information: "They wrapped them up separately, you know . . . *organs*."

"Yes, I know," said Marianne. "They put them in jars."

"Not those sort of organs . . . *other* sorts."

"What other sorts?"

"Penises," said Mary-Jane.

An elderly lady standing nearby raised her head to stare. Marianne began to feel uncomfortable. She turned away, before she could start blushing.

"Let's go and find those marbles."

Mary-Jane giggled and said, "Yes, let's" as if there were something funny about it. On their way to the marbles they passed a naked statue. Mary-Jane poked her in the side and said, "Hey, look! Remind you of anyone?"

Trying to be flip, to show her sophistication, she said, "Paul Newman?"

"Paul Newman!" Mary-Jane doubled up. "When did you see Paul Newman?"

"I've seen Paul Newman."

"Not like that, you haven't. Wonder what the Bunny Rabbit would say if we petitioned for one in the playground?"

"Be overjoyed, I shouldn't wonder. After all, it's Art, isn't it?"

Mary-Jane giggled again. "Is that what you call it?"

Marianne said, "Pornography is in the eye of the beholder" and moved on. It was beginning to embarrass her, goggling at naked statues. It was so patently obvious what one was goggling at. Mary-Jane, like a leech, stuck with her.

"Hey, Marianne," she said. She plucked confidentially at her arm. "What's it like? With Abe?"

What did she mean, what was it like? "What is what like?" said Marianne.

"You know!"

No, she thought, I do not know. I don't want to know. Just shut up and go away and stop polluting everything. She shook her head so that her hair fell over her face. "What are you talking about?"

"Doing it . . . with someone who can't see. Does it make any difference?"

Coldly, with her hair over her face, she said, "Why should it make any difference? Just because he can't see, that doesn't make him a freak, does it?"

"I didn't mean that," said Mary-Jane. "I only meant—"

"Oh, shut up!" said Marianne. "You bore me!"

One-track mind, that was all that woman had, and she loathed it when people implied that because Abe was blind there must be other things wrong with him too. They did it all the time, in shops, in bus lines, in eating places, not meaning to, not even thinking about it, automatically addressing themselves to her instead of him—"What size does he take? What color does he want? Shall I cut things up for him?"—as if he were slow on the uptake and couldn't answer for himself. Abe shrugged his shoulders and said, "Oh, you get used to it," but she didn't think she ever would.

She left Mary-Jane in an offended huff and went off to look at the marbles without her. She had had enough of the Mountain and her insinuations for one day.

When she arrived home there wasn't any water coming out of the cold-water tap. She yelled out of the kitchen window at her mother, "What's happened to the water?"

Mrs. Fenton, looking up from her desultory weeding of the one flowerbed (so-called) said, "It's been turned off.

You're back earlier than I thought. . . . I'll get tea in a minute. Abe's just putting a new washer on the bathroom tap."

"Can he manage?" said Marianne.

"I presume so." Prosaically, Mrs. Fenton returned to her weeding. "He wouldn't have offered if he couldn't."

No, thought Marianne, I suppose he wouldn't. She looked at her mother, bent over the flowerbed, and felt a rare surge of affection. Why couldn't everyone treat Abe like that? As a man no different from any other man? Perfectly capable of putting washers on taps and removing lids from jars of marmalade and knocking nails into walls and—and everything else as well? She thought of Mary-Jane and thought, I hate her. She looked again at her mother and thought, Abe's right. I oughtn't to grumble. She really *isn't* as bad as all that.

In fact, life at home had been transformed along with life at school. Her mother hardly ever seemed to nag at all these days, and even on occasion addressed her as an equal, consulting her views, asking her advice.

"What color shall we get the house done? I'm tired of green and cream. Suppose we had something different for a change? What about yellow? Or something mad and outrageous? Purple, or turquoise . . . what do you feel?"

The first serious falling-out they had didn't come until just after Primrose Adcock Day, and even then it was more in the nature of a civilized difference of opinion than a full-blooded row. Mrs. Fenton said, "I didn't say anything during the heat wave, but I do think, now that we're back to normal, that it would be better if you *didn't* run in and out of the bathroom wearing nothing but your underclothes—and you don't have to roll your eyes at me like that. I'm perfectly well aware that Abe can't see you, but I would still prefer it if you didn't. It surely isn't all that much to ask?"

For the sake of peace, she gave way. It was the most futile thing she had ever heard, but who was she to ruin a good relationship? From then on she wore her bathrobe, as if she were living in a hotel. It didn't stop her grumbling to Abe about it, the following Tuesday, as they washed up together after a meal of salad and fresh fruit in his room. Abe, taking her mother's side as usual, said, "Absolutely right! I don't run around in *my* underwear, why should you run around in yours?"

"Well, why shouldn't I? This dish is *filthy*. I don't see why everyone shouldn't go around stark naked, if that's what they feel like doing."

"Heaven forbid! What a ghastly thought!"

"What's ghastly about it? Apart from the weather?"

"All those flabby thighs and great wobbling behinds?"

"Well, you wouldn't have to see them."

"No, but I'd have to feel them—that would be even worse! Imagine it on a crowded bus . . . a vast mass of quivering humanity all wedged up together like a big corporate jelly. This any better?"

She took back the newly washed dish. "It'll do." It still had a dirty rim around the edge, but she didn't tell him; she simply wiped it off with the tea towel. After all, what did it really matter? "*I* think," she said, "that it would be a good thing. Break down inhibitions if everyone knew what everyone else looked like."

"Do you *want* to know what everyone else looks like?"

Thoughts, unbidden, of naked statues sprang to her mind. She didn't know why it was, but ever since Primrose Adcock Day it had become increasingly difficult to keep naked statues *out* of her mind. Everywhere she went she seemed to see them. They rose up before her at the most inopportune moments— like now, with Abe, doing the dishes.

She said aggressively, "Well, why not?"

"I should think it would be one big turn-off, that's why not!"

She scowled. "Do you think *I* would be one big turn-off?"

"Ah! Now we're getting personal," said Abe. He pulled the plug out of the sink, turned, bumped into her, steadied himself, said, "Of course you wouldn't: *you*'re not fat and flabby," snatched up a towel and walked across to the radio. "What's the time?"

"Just eight. How do you know that I'm not?"

"Oh, now, come on! I know what you look like. Listen: what's this?"

"Haydn? Mozart? *How* do you know?"

"I'm not stupid—and you're just guessing." He threw himself down into the room's only armchair, hooking one leg over the side. "Nothing like Haydn or Mozart. Try again."

She said at random, "Beethoven, Brahms—"

"Which Beethoven-Brahms?"

"*I* don't know . . . Fifth?"

"Fifth! It's Beethoven's Choral. You ought to be ashamed of yourself. Leave that lot. Come over here and listen."

She wasn't in a mood for listening to music. Sometimes she was; but this evening she wasn't. She sat on the floor by the side of Abe's chair, with her legs hugged in to her chest and her chin resting on her knees, and tried obediently to concentrate, but it wasn't any use: naked statues kept obtruding. This is dreadful, she thought. She was turning into some kind of sex maniac. She sprang around and said,

"Abe . . . when are you going to start teaching me Braille?"

"Some time."

"During my vacation?"

"If you like."

"Promise?"

"Anything to keep you quiet. Come here!" He unhooked his leg, hoisted her up off the floor. "Concentrate on Beethoven."

How could she concentrate on Beethoven when her mind was full of naked statues? She wished she had never gone to the British Museum in the first place—she wished that Mary-Jane had never gone. It was all her fault. Putting ideas into her head, making her think of things she'd never thought of before and didn't want to think of now. As for all that prudish nonsense about not running in and out of the bathroom in her underwear—what was the difference between bra and panties and a bikini? No difference at all. If anything the bikini was worse, because it was last year's and she'd grown out of it. She ought by rights to have had a new one, except that—

"What's the problem?" said Abe. "Have you got a tummy ache?"

"No—"

"So what's the matter? What do you keep wriggling for? Don't you like Beethoven?"

"Yes!" She adored Beethoven. Heavenly, beautiful Beethoven . . . "Why have you got hair on your chest?" she said. "Stephen hasn't."

"That's because Stephen is only a callow youth."

"He's not a callow youth! He's seventeen, and he's a lot bigger than you are."

"That's right: denigrate me."

"I'm not denigrating you." She ran a finger up the center of his chest. "Just struck me as odd, that's all."

"Something else will strike you as odd if you're not very careful." Firmly, he imprisoned her hand in his. "You do realize," he said, "that you're asking for trouble?"

She was about to ask him "What sort of trouble?" but she wasn't given the chance. Before she could even frame the words, the door was flung open and her mother was there saying: "For goodness' sake! Are you two *deaf*, or—"

A sort of silence came over the room. Beethoven went on playing, but still there was a silence. Marianne wriggled to her feet. Abe said, "Turn the radio down." She did so.

"What's the matter?" she said. Why the sudden atmosphere? They hadn't been doing anything wrong, only listening to music. She could hardly complain about the neighbors, it wasn't even nine o'clock. Anyway, she never came back from bridge until half-past ten. "Why are you back so early?" she asked.

"Mrs. Curry wasn't feeling well. She had to go home. Abe, I wonder, could you come and see if you can manage to open the front door for me? I've got the key in, but it won't turn. I don't know if it simply needs brute force, or—"

"Surely," said Abe.

"It could be it needs a new lock. It's been going funny for some time."

"So how did you get in?" said Marianne.

"I climbed through the kitchen window, which *you* had left gaping open. I've been ringing at the bell for the past fifteen minutes. I was getting in quite a panic. I could hear the radio was on. I was beginning to have visions that you'd gone out and that Abe had had some ghastly accident."

"It's that silly chiming thing," said Marianne. "It doesn't

penetrate. You ought to have a proper buzzer. We'd have heard that."

"Oh, would you?" her mother retorted.

"Well, of course we would. The radio wasn't *loud*."

It was no use blaming them for the fact that she had a stupid ding-dong thing instead of a real bell. Ding dong! It was like garden gnomes and ducks on the wall. She followed her mother down the stairs. Abe, after some manipulation, got the front door open and said he thought the mechanism had gone.

"So it needs a new lock." Her mother sounded weary, as if everything, suddenly, was too much—as if having to have a new lock put on the front door was the last straw.

Abe went back upstairs. Marianne, for want of anything better to do, went into the kitchen and made a cup of tea. Somehow she didn't like to suggest that she go back up with Abe to finish listening to Beethoven. She couldn't have said why, but she felt instinctively that it would be frowned upon. For the next hour she sat slumped on the sofa in the front room, glaze-eyed before the television. Her mother stayed in the kitchen drinking tea and brooding over the thought of what a new lock was going to cost—at least, she presumed that was what it was she was brooding over. When she went out to raid the cookie jar she found her sitting at the kitchen table smoking a cigarette, which was something she only ever gave way to in moments of dire stress, such as when the final demand for the taxes happened to coincide with a threatening letter from the gas company or the telephone was about to be cut off and the school fees hadn't been paid yet. Normally, because of the school fees, she wasn't sympathetic. Tonight, trying hard, she said, "Perhaps Abe might be able to do it? If I helped him . . . it would at least save labor costs." Her mother, still sounding weary, said, "Don't be silly. Go back and watch television." Affronted, she did so.

A few minutes later she heard her mother go upstairs. She heard her knock at Abe's door and the door open, and then she heard footsteps overhead and the low buzz of voices. Decided after all to ask him about the lock, had she? There wasn't the least reason why Abe shouldn't be able to put a lock on a front door as well as the next person—not if she told him where to drill the holes, or whatever it was one had to do. Between them they could manage it.

A yawn engulfed her, nearly turning her face inside out. This stuff on the television was really boring, but *boring*. She switched through all three channels, trying a bit of this and a bit of that. It was all boring. In the end she turned off completely. Quarter-past ten. Her mother had been up there with Abe for nearly twenty minutes. What on earth were they finding to talk about? It seemed an inordinately long time to be asking him whether he could fix a new lock.

She stifled another yawn before it could take her head right off. She might just as well go to bed and read a book as sit down here doing nothing. Whatever it was that was going on, Abe would tell her about it in the morning.

16

>>>

ABE WASN'T THERE IN THE MORNING. SHE GALLOPED DOWN to breakfast quarter of an hour late, just as she always did, and he wasn't there. Only her mother, eating bacon and eggs. "Where's Abe?" said Marianne. "Isn't he up?"

"He's already left, he had to be in early. You'll find your bacon under the broiler."

Frowning as she fetched the bacon, by now half cold, she said, "He didn't tell me."

"He doesn't tell you everything. Incidentally, you may or may not be pleased to hear that after this semester we'll be having the house to ourselves once again."

"What?"

She froze in her tracks in the middle of the floor. Her mother, with a calm that even she could see was assumed for the occasion, reached over for the teapot.

"I've decided against any more lodgers—definite, this time. As a matter of fact, I'm seriously thinking of putting the house up for sale and going for something smaller. I thought perhaps an apartment. It would really be far more convenient. What do you think?"

Trembling, she set down her plate. In a voice that was only just under control, she said, "What's happening to Abe?"

"He's planning to look for somewhere else—probably go

for an apartment himself. Now that he's learned how to manage. This was only a temporary arrangement, just until he found his feet. You couldn't expect him to go on living in a bed-sitter indefinitely."

"You've turned him out—" She stared at her mother, incredulous, accusing. "You've *turned him out!*"

"Don't be silly, of course I haven't turned him out. He'll be here until the end of the semester, and then—"

"That's barely two weeks away! How's he going to find somewhere in two weeks?"

"Well, I imagine he'll be going back to his sister for the holidays, so—"

"He won't! He wasn't! He was going to stay here and work! He was going to teach me Braille! How can he go off and live in an apartment all by himself?"

"I didn't say he was necessarily going to be all by himself."

"So who's he going to live with?"

"Oh, I'm sure he'll find someone. Someone from school, or—"

"They're all women at his school!"

"Well"—her mother spoke with determined cheerfulness —"it's supposed to be quite the thing these days, isn't it? Members of the opposite sex shacking up together. Isn't that the expression? Get on with your breakfast, you'll be late for school."

She couldn't get on with her breakfast. The food choked her, and she could scarcely see it for the gathering tears. "You told him to go—last night! You *told* him."

"We discussed it; he agreed with me."

"What do you mean, he *agreed* with you?"

"That it might be best. I hadn't realized how far sound can carry in these old houses, especially the sound of a piano. The people next door have been very patient, but they do have two small children to consider. It's not fair on them."

"It's not fair on Abe!" She knew perfectly well that the two small children had nothing to do with it, nor the sound of the piano. It was her mother, for reasons of her own, wanting to get rid of him. "I just don't see how you *can*—I don't know how you can be so *cruel*. As if he hasn't got enough to put up with without people like you"—the tears came in a sudden spurt—"people like you k-kicking him in the t-teeth—"

"No one is kicking him in the teeth. We had a perfectly friendly discussion and we came to an agreement. Now I suggest, if you're not going to eat that breakfast, that you wash your face and go off to school and forget about it. If you carry on like this I shall begin to think it was a mistake ever to have had him here in the first place."

"*I* told *you* that," said Marianne, "right at the beginning!"

A day at school had never seemed so long. Fortunately, with exams over and the end of the semester only two weeks away (two weeks! Only two weeks, and then Abe would be gone) discipline was somewhat relaxed and nobody took her to task for not concentrating. During the lunch break she was on corridor duty. She stood like a traffic policeman in the main entrance hall droning "Single file" and "Don't run" and thinking all the time, She's turned him out—she's turned him *out*.

Beth Walker came up and said, "I've just gone around you three times in a circle and you never even noticed. I say, are you all right?"

She said: "Yes, of course" because that was what one did say, unless one happened to be Emily Rivers-Smith, who gloried in every least little thing, but the blood was pounding in her ears like waves on the seashore and her eyes were hot and burning from the constant effort of keeping back tears.

Immediately at four o'clock, ignoring a written instruction that had been on the bulletin board for a week to the effect that all members of the senior high were to remain behind for a special Speech Day briefing, she snatched up her briefcase, crammed her hat on her head, and ran. Ten minutes later, breathless, she cantered up the hill to Rosemount. Abe was on his way down, accompanied by Hilary.

"Hallo!" he said. "You nearly missed me—I thought you had a meeting?"

"Didn't go."

"You'll be in trouble!"

Hilary, abandoning Abe to Marianne, said, "I'll dash if you don't mind . . . see you tomorrow." As she swung off down the hill, Abe felt for Marianne's hand. He held it very tightly but didn't say anything. For the first hundred yards they walked in silence, then: *"Why?"* Marianne asked, and her voice came out all ugly and contorted, twisted with tears from a throat that was tied into knots. "Abe, *why?"*

He didn't ask her, Why what? He said, "Not here. Take me somewhere we can sit and talk."

She took him to the town hall gardens, deserted at this hour with most people homeward bound. There they sat on a park bench, in an alcove, with a purple wisteria climbing the wall behind them, and Abe did his best to tell her why.

"I think she feels—perhaps—that it's not good for you . . . to be quite so . . . friendly with me."

"Not *good* for me?" She was flabbergasted. How could it possibly be not good for her? It was Abe who had given her direction in life—who had taught her that she could sing, that she could mix with people, that she wasn't the oddity they had all thought her. "Not *good* for me?" she repeated.

"I guess we have to try and see it from her point of view. After all, I am eight years older than you are—"

"Seven and a half! Anyway, what's age got to do with it?"

"Oh, now, come on! Don't be naïve! A man of twenty-four and a girl of sixteen?"

"People can be married, you know, at sixteen!"

"Yes," said Abe, "and some people have to be."

The ready blush sprang to her cheeks. "But we've never—"

"No, I know we've never, but we just *might*, mightn't we?"

Bitterly she said, "If she didn't want me to get friendly with you, why did she let you have the room in the first place?"

"I imagine because she thought that being blind I would be safe to have around . . . like some kind of pet eunuch."

"That's obscene!"

"Shattering to my ego, certainly. I wouldn't exactly call it obscene."

"Well, it is! It's like saying that just because you can't see, you can't—"

"Yes," said Abe. "Well, people do, don't they?"

"They don't! I don't!"

"You did at first."

"I did not!"

"Well, all right, so you didn't actually go so far as to think I was a mental deficient, but you were pretty damn sure I wasn't the same as everyone else! The old kid-glove treatment, wasn't it?"

"That was only because I didn't know!"

"What didn't you know?"

"How to—"

"How to treat me? It didn't occur to you, I suppose, to treat me just as you would any normal human being?"

The tears that had been threatening all day came with a spurt, self-pityingly, to her eyes. "That's not fair!"

"Why is it not fair? Because I'm *not* a normal human being? Oh, Marianne!" He pulled her towards him, an arm about her shoulders. "I'm sorry! Forgive me—I've no right to go on at you. It's not your fault."

"No," she said, savagely, "it's hers! Going and ruining everything with her horrid pr-rurient m-mind and beastly f-fantasies."

"Hush!" said Abe. His fingers found the elastic band that kept her hair in place. He pulled it off, so that the thick, honey-colored strands fell about her shoulders. "It's not the end of the world. I'll still be around. We can still see each other."

"But it won't be the *same*."

"No; it won't be the same—but things rarely do stay the same for very long. They tend to change whether one likes it or not. Another year and you'll be off to college, and that will be another change."

She wiped the back of her hand across her nose. "I shall go to one in London."

"Well, we shall see," said Abe. "In the meantime, there's still our two weeks down in Devon. Don't forget that. That's something to look forward to."

"If she still lets me."

"Oh, she'll still let you—so long as we don't go doing anything silly. She doesn't want you not to see me at all, she just doesn't want us to be—quite so much on top of each other."

She didn't want them to listen to Beethoven and cook

omelettes. She didn't want Marianne "running in and out of the bathroom in her underwear." She would be able to run in and out of the bathroom in her underwear as much as she liked from now on.

"It won't be anywhere near as bad as you think," said Abe. "I promise you."

"But where"—she felt in her pocket for a handkerchief— "where are you going to go? What are you going to do?"

"I'm not going back home, that's for sure. Someone was telling me there's a small hotel-cum-guesthouse just down the road from school—I'll probably try there for starters. Then maybe an apartment—"

"But who with? You can't live on your own!"

"No? I don't see why not—other people do. And you don't have to tell me that I'm not other people! I'm perfectly well aware of the difficulties—more now than I was before. But if it sets your mind at rest, there's a good possibility I might be able to talk Donald into taking me on. You remember Donald?"

"Your friend from college—the one who gave the Mozart recital."

"That's right. Well, he's on the look-out for a place right now. It's just a question of whether I can manage to convince him that the south of London is as good as the north. He's quite willing to have me share with him. Now why the big sigh? Imagine how much better when you can come and see me in my own pad. We could even give a party—you'd like that, wouldn't you?"

She didn't say again that it wouldn't be the same. She even, dimly and with a certain reluctance, began to perceive that it might almost be fun.

"So there you are," said Abe. "Not as bad as you thought."

He pulled her to her feet. "One last word of advice," he said. "Don't go having things out with your mother. You'll only lose your temper, and it won't help. Just play it cool. Hang loose, let it all happen . . . things will work out. You'll see."

17

>>>

ALL THE LOVELY BRIGHT HAPPINESS HAD GONE. ABE STAYED on until the end of the semester, but it was not the same as it had been. Mrs. Fenton didn't go to bridge anymore on Tuesday evenings. She said the group had broken up for the summer, as if it were a school, and that they would "re-form later on." Marianne knew that by later on she meant when Abe was safely off the premises.

Relations with her mother had become strained once more. They addressed each other formally, with exaggerated politeness: "I wonder if you would terribly mind" and "I do beg your pardon" and "Just so long as it isn't going to inconvenience you." Beneath the politeness, her mother was wary, waiting for trouble; Marianne hostile, spoiling for a row. The tension between them crackled and sparked: it needed but one word out of place to set it alight.

Even Abe, normally so easy-going, seemed to have caught the prevailing mood and become tense and prickly—like a hedgehog (as Marianne was unwise enough to inform him) with an attack of shingles. Once such a remark would have made him laugh and make a face. Now he only snapped at her, "It's not Making-Fun-of-the-Handicapped Week, is it? Not as far as I know." Admittedly he had just tripped over her hockey stick for the third time in as many days; but all the same, it was not like Abe.

On Sunday he went up to town to spend the day with his sister. Marianne said wistfully, "Can I walk up to the station with you?" and as she saw him on to the train, "Can I come and meet you again this evening?"

"I shouldn't bother," said Abe. "I probably won't be back till late."

"Doesn't matter. Doesn't get dark till late."

"No, well, I still wouldn't like the thought of you hanging around."

"I wouldn't have to hang around—we could arrange a time. If you said you were going to catch a train about nine o'clock—"

"Yes, but I couldn't guarantee."

"Oh." She bit her lip. "Well, I—I could just wander up anyway. Say about ten—"

"And suppose I didn't get back till midnight? Don't worry, I'll find my own way. I can always jump in a cab."

Her cheeks crimsoned. He didn't want her to come to meet him—he was making it quite obvious. He just wanted her to leave him alone. If it hadn't been for her, he wouldn't be being thrown out of his room. She turned, began blundering back up the platform. Abe called after her. "Marianne! What are you—" She didn't hear the rest. Someone blew a whistle and the train started to pull out. When she looked back, Abe had gone.

Quite impossible to spend the rest of the day at home, in company with her mother. She had promised Abe that there wouldn't be any scenes. She had given him her word, "no having things out." She knew if she stayed indoors the temptation would be too great.

Mrs. Fenton, when she arrived back, was upstairs with the vacuum cleaner. Marianne helped herself to some fruit and cookies, took a bottle of milk from the refrigerator, left a hastily scribbled note on the kitchen table—*Gone for a ride*—grabbed her bicycle from the shed, and went.

When she arrived back for the second time it was four o'clock and her own note was propped against a cup and saucer with an addition in her mother's handwriting: *Dinner in oven, just needs heating up. Over the road with Peggy, back about 7.* That, she thought, was the way she and her mother ought to communicate just at the moment. It saved any possibility of unpleasantness.

Punctually at seven Mrs. Fenton returned. She was in one of her brisk, determined-to-please-at-all-costs and pretend-there's-nothing-wrong moods. She said: "Did you get your dinner?" and "What time did you get in?" and "Abe telephoned you earlier."

"Abe? When?"

"This morning. About eleven. He said he'd try again; I don't know if he did, I went over to Peggy's. Do you want a cup of coffee?"

At nine o'clock, when she was sitting half-asleep in front of the television, too inert to get up and do anything else, Abe called again.

"I'm here," he said. "At the station . . . coming to collect me?"

The following Friday, the semester came to an end; the next day, after lunch, Abe moved out. He couldn't take his piano to the Briarley Guesthouse, so Mrs. Fenton had said he was welcome to leave it where it was until such time as he had found an apartment. She had also said that of course Marianne could give him a hand with his things and help him settle in,

"But I want you back here no later than five. There's dinner to prepare."

Tonight of all nights she had had to go and ask the Peggy woman to come and eat with them. Marianne didn't like the Peggy woman. She was a widow and genteel and had come down in the world. She had recently moved south from Leamington Spa and had a son called Simon who was studying mathematics at Cambridge and was reputed to be brilliant. She couldn't stand people whose children were brilliant, especially when they never ceased telling you about it—and why, for heaven's sake, did they have to have her over for dinner? They never had people over for dinner. Why her? Why tonight?

"Because it's Simon's first night home," said Mrs. Fenton.

"*Simon*? That creep? You mean she's bringing *him*?"

She knew then that it was all part of a plot. They wanted her to gaze upon this wet mathematical genius and think how wonderful he was. Anything to lure her away from Abe. Mrs. Fenton said, "It'll be someone for you to talk to. He'll be able to tell you what it's like, being at college."

"And what the square root of 5,001 is, and how to work out the area of a pyramid. . . . Perhaps he might even entertain us with logarithm tables."

Her mother looked at her sharply. "I shall expect you to be polite to him."

"Oh, I shall be *polite*," said Marianne. "Just don't expect me to enthuse, that's all."

The Briarley Guesthouse was two houses turned into one, with the front gardens cemented over for cars and gruesome orange shutters at the windows. It catered mainly to traveling salesmen. Marianne caught a glimpse of a dining room laid out with individual tables, each with its own cruet and bottle of HP Sauce, and a lounge with television set and plastic armchairs. In the entrance hall was a pay telephone and a glass door marked PRIVATE. Through this glass door the proprietress came to meet them. She seemed pleasant, in spite of obviously having an eye for business and wearing aggressive purple glasses with frosted wings. If she addressed herself to Marianne rather than to Abe ("He'll only have to ring if he wants anything. I've put him next door to the bathroom. Does he take tea in the mornings?") it was no more than one had grown to expect. People stopped doing it after a while, once they had come to know him. Abe said it was embarrassment as much as anything else.

The room next door to the bathroom was drab and bare. Just a bed and a chair, a wardrobe, chest of drawers and table. There wasn't even a gas ring for making tea; not even a picture on the wall. It was probably no worse than any other room in any other guesthouse, but still it was depressing. She was glad for once that Abe couldn't see what surrounded him. In spite of it, he obviously sensed something of the atmosphere, or maybe it was there in the tone of her voice as she showed him around—"chest of drawers . . . *ward*robe . . . thing for putting suitcases on . . ." She never had been good at hiding her feelings; maybe it was she herself who gave it away. Whatever it was, as they came back full circle, back to the chest of drawers, Abe pulled down the corners of his mouth and said, "Not exactly home away from home, I take it."

"They just don't try," said Marianne. "It would be so easy . . . all it needs is a bit of imagination."

"I don't expect anyone ever stays here long enough to bother—and neither shall I be, if I can help it. First thing Monday morning, it's out apartment hunting."

Yes; that was another sore point. First thing Monday

morning she would be reporting to the local supermarket. Her mother had said that if she wanted two weeks down in Devon she must make a contribution, so for the next month she was going to be on the checkout, taking people's money. At the time, she hadn't argued with the fairness of it, but she hadn't known then that Abe was going to be thrown out of his room and have to start looking for somewhere else. It did nothing to quell the pangs of her disgruntlement to know that while she was sitting under artificial lighting stabbing at a cash register and putting things in plastic bags, it was going to be Hilary, in her mother's Mini, who was taking Abe on his apartment hunt. At least his friend Donald had finally agreed that the south of London was just as good as the north. That was some consolation. He had said that if Abe came up with a suitable place, he was "willing to run the risk of sharing with me"—though for her part she couldn't see what risk there was supposed to be. *She* wouldn't have minded sharing with him.

"Cheer up," said Abe. "Don't do a Gloomfest on me. . . . Show me where I telephone for help, then show me where the bathroom is, then let's go and have a coffee somewhere."

She left him at the front door of the Briarley at quarter to five.

"See you tomorrow?" she said. "For rehearsal?"

"But, sweetheart, there isn't any rehearsal—"

Rehearsals had been called off for the vacation period because too many people at too many different times were going to be away—Ginny up in Scotland, Graham on the Norfolk Broads, Hilary in Austria. Even Stephen was being "dragged off to some flaming seaside bordello for a week of clear soup and semolina pudding." Only Abe and Marianne were staying put.

"You know," Abe said gently, "that Thursday was the last until—"

"Yes, I know! But *we* still could, couldn't we? We could work on something—" She scanned his face anxiously. It wasn't always easy with Abe to tell what thoughts were going through his mind; you couldn't read it in his eyes, as you could with other people. "We could have a go at 'White as Lilies.' That bit where I always—"

"Where?" said Abe.

"Where I always go flat: 'Quitting faith with foul dis—'"

"Yes, but where?"

She held her breath. "Here?"

For a minute she thought he was going to say no, it wouldn't be right; or no, her mother wouldn't like it; or just simply no.

"Would they allow it?" he said.

"Why shouldn't they?"

"They sometimes have rules about these things: no guests allowed in rooms—especially young lady guests."

"Well, but we could tell her I'd—I'd come to read the paper to you, come to write a letter for you—she couldn't object to *that*."

Abe seemed doubtful.

"Well, she couldn't! It wouldn't be human!"

"I suppose we could give it a go—but only on one condition: no cloak-and-dagger stuff. I don't want you sneaking off saying you're going for a ride, or meeting a school friend, or—"

"I won't!" She had in fact been going to do exactly that, but no matter; she would find a way around it.

"You'll tell her the truth?"

"I'll tell her."

"You promise?"

"I promise."

"So when shall I see you?"

Her heart lifted. "I'll come over first thing after lunch—same time as for rehearsals."

"Always assuming your mother says yes—but whatever she says, whether it's yes or whether it's no, for God's sake don't start arguing the toss, because it's just not worth it. Just bite your tongue and put up with it—and don't make faces at me!" He pressed a finger against her nose. "I know you think I'm being an old woman, but sooner put up with a few restrictions now than a total ban later on. Just bear one thing in mind: it may be all very easy for you to go out and replace *me*; it wouldn't be so easy for me to go out and find another you. You just remember that when you're tempted to go pitching into battle . . . try thinking of me for once instead of yourself!"

That evening, toward the end of dinner, when the Peggy woman had exhausted herself saying how brilliantly Simon was doing at Cambridge and Simon (to give him his due) had exhausted himself trying to crawl under the table and get away from it, she was horrified to hear her mother say, "If you're not doing anything tomorrow, why not get Marianne to show you around? She's got all sorts of secret places she goes off to."

She swallowed urgently. "I've got a rehearsal tomorrow!"

"You're always having rehearsals. Surely you can skip one for once?"

"No! I can't! They're important!" Her mother drew her eyebrows together. It was a warning sign. Remembering Abe's injunction, she added hastily, "I'd love to show you around, I really would. It's just that we've got this concert, and—"

"That's okay," said Simon. "I've got something on anyway."

She had the feeling he was as relieved as she was. Beyond the math exam they had absolutely nothing whatsoever in common.

Afterward, alone with her mother, she said, "I suppose I *am* allowed to go and rehearse tomorrow? Or do you think I might meet up with a mad rapist in the street?"

Her mother said, "I'll tell you one thing I think: that is, that if you take that tone of voice with me, my girl, you're going to find yourself not being allowed to go and do anything tomorrow. You may be sixteen, but while you're living under my roof you'll adopt my code of behavior. Heavy sarcasm is what I can do without. I sometimes think the trouble with you is that you've been given too much leeway."

She bit back the retort that rose to her tongue. "For God's sake," Abe had said, "don't start arguing the toss . . . try thinking of me for once instead of yourself." After a moment of struggle, thinking of him very hard indeed, she said: "Sorry. Didn't mean it. Do the washing-up if you like—act of penance."

At least she hadn't been banned from going to rehearsal.

18

‗‗‗‗‗‗‗‗‗‗‗‗‗‗‗‗‗‗‗‗‗‗‗‗‗‗‗‗‗‗‗‗‗‗‗‗‗‗

NEXT DAY, JUST AS SHE WAS ON THE POINT OF LEAVING, HER mother said, "Where was it you said these rehearsals took place?"

Marianne froze.

"Over at Hilary's." Just to cover herself, she added, "Usually."

"And where is Hilary's?"

"She lives up near Lloyd Park—one of the big houses."

"I see. Money."

"Yes, well—it's what you'd expect, isn't it? She goes to Rosemount. They don't let just anyone in there. None of your common council house people. None of your riff-raff. Got to keep up the tone of the place."

"Oh, get on with you!" Exasperated but good-natured, her mother opened the door. "Jump on your hobby horse and be off . . . what time shall I expect you back?"

She hesitated. "Six?"

"All right, no later. I'll have dinner on the table."

She felt just a few twinges of guilt as she caught the bus into town and got off at the Briarley, but not so very many. After all, it wasn't as if she were doing anything wrong. She hadn't actually *said* that she was going to Hilary's. All those nervous glances were quite unnecessary: no one was trailing her in false beard and moustache.

The proprietress, whose name was Mrs. Busby, was seated at the reception desk. Marianne said, "Is it all right if I go up to Mr. Shonfeld? I've brought the paper to read to him."

She had stopped at a newsstand on the way and bought a copy of the *Guardian*, plus a music magazine that she knew he liked. Mrs. Busby said, "That's all right, dear. You go up. Are you a Helpmate?"

Confused, she said, "No, just a friend." (It was only much later she discovered that "Helpmates" were a bunch of local senior high students who went around doing things for old ladies and taking blind people for walks.) Mrs. Busby said that friend or Helpmate, she could still go up.

"He needs a bit of company, young fellow like that. Shame, isn't it?"

Marianne agreed that it was. She found Abe listening to music on the radio. He said, "Did you ask her?"

"Mrs. Busby?"

"Your mother."

"Oh. Her. Yes, of course I did. I've brought you the *Guardian* and a music magazine. There's an article about your friend Donald . . . do you want me to read it?"

She read for about an hour, until Abe said she would make herself hoarse if she did any more and suppose they went out and had a coffee somewhere. They had coffee at the same place as they had had it the day before. It was only fifty yards down the road from the Briarley. Abe said that this evening he was planning to venture there "all by myself. I don't think even I could manage to get lost over such a short distance as that." She didn't like the idea of his having to go there by himself. Not that anything was likely to happen to him—there weren't any major roads to be crossed or hazards to negotiate—but it seemed such a lonely thing to do—her sitting at home being bored, Abe drinking coffee by himself. It was all so ridiculous and unnecessary.

After the coffee they went for a stroll round the town hall gardens. It wasn't very exciting, but at least it was exercise and better than staying indoors. Abe said that this morning he had walked up and down the hill to Rosemount three times. "It's the only route I'm absolutely certain of." He laughed as he said it, but she didn't laugh with him. She didn't think it very funny, Abe having to walk up and down the same stretch of road. If it weren't for her mother and her lurid mind, they could have gone out to the Kingdom and had a proper walk.

They went back to the Briarley, which seemed more depressing than ever after the outside world, and for the last hour they played Scrabble, sitting on the floor because there was only one chair. When the time came for her to leave, Abe insisted on walking to the bus with her. She tried to talk him out of it—she would rather have said good-bye to him in private than out there, in public—but he brushed all objections aside.

"Good God, if I can't find my own way back by this time . . . I've been using the stop for the past semester and a half!"

She forbore to point out that he had always had either herself or someone from school to take him there, to see him safely across the main road. She knew that he wouldn't want her to. If she started agitating about main roads, she would be putting herself in the category of people who fussed. As they parted he said, "Chin up! I'll call you Monday evening—let you know how the apartment hunt's progressing. You just keep your fingers crossed."

When she got home, tea was ready and waiting. There were special peach preserves and cakes from the baker. Her mother was trying very hard. She said, "Have a good rehearsal?"

She needn't think peach preserves and fancy cakes made up for the loss of Abe. "Yes, thank you," said Marianne. She said it without a qualm. It's her own fault, she thought; her own fault entirely. "What are we celebrating?" she said. "Having the house to ourselves once again?"

On Thursday when she went to see Abe it was raining so hard that a walk was out of the question. She read aloud for a bit and they played some more Scrabble and twiddled with the knobs on the radio in pursuit of something worth listening to, and finally, in desperation, braved the downpour and ran the fifty yards to the coffee bar. Abe was so sure of the way by now that he didn't mind running. The waitresses all greeted him as an old friend. She thought that he must spend a lot of his time in that coffee bar.

He asked her how the cash registers were going, and she said, "Boring but bearable. What about the apartment hunt?" He confessed that the hunt was proving more difficult than he had anticipated. So far he had found only one place that could be said to be suitable—"but unfortunately *I* wasn't suitable for *it*. The minute we turned up they took one look at me and said no."

She was indignant. "What do you mean, they said no?"

"No. N-O. No blacks, no babies, no blind."

"You're not *serious*?"

"They thought I'd be too much of a fire risk."

"Abe, you're *not* serious?"

"Well, at any rate, they didn't want me. Don't worry, we'll keep on looking."

She stared at him anxiously. "But Hilary's going to be away next week. How will you m—"

"Steve's volunteered. Says he's going to come and pick me up on his bike and we're going to comb the district. Have faith! You can't expect everything to fall into your lap all at once."

On Saturday it was still raining. After the usual reading session they played a bit of Scrabble, but Scrabble, by now, was beginning to pall. The radio was all light music, and if there was one thing calculated to rouse Abe to intolerance it was light music. He said he would rather have raucous pop than candyfloss, but when she turned over to Radio One he said it insulted the intelligence and for God's sake to get rid of it. On a flash of inspiration she suggested he might start teaching her Braille.

"What, now?"

"Why not?"

"Because it's hard work, that's why not. Still, if you really want—"

After only ten minutes she wasn't at all sure that she did really want. Maybe a guesthouse bedroom was not the ideal setting, but she didn't see how she was ever going to master all those different combinations of dots, and even if she did, she didn't see how she was ever going to be able to feel them with her fingertips. Abe gave her a sheet of Braille paper, all thick and brown and cardboardy, on which he had typed out the alphabet for her on the special machine he used for making teaching notes. He said, "There you are. See what you can do with that." She couldn't do anything with it. If she closed her eyes it just felt like random dots on the paper. Abe told her not to press too hard or she would wear them flat and then there wouldn't be anything there to feel anyway, but if she didn't press hard the dots weren't even dots but only vague bumps. She had watched Abe reading Braille. He moved his fingers across the page at a speed that now seemed to her quite incredible. He said it was the result of twenty years' experience and she mustn't be discouraged; but when, in a small voice, she suggested it might perhaps be a good idea to postpone the teaching of Braille till another day, he made no demur and he read her no lectures.

"So what do you want to do, then?" he said.

"We could try a walk—it's not coming down as much as it was."

They trod a sodden path to the town hall gardens—there really wasn't anywhere else they could go. The country was too far, and the only municipal parks were hefty bus rides away, and who wanted to trail around municipal parks on a soaking-wet day? It was being brought home to her, as never before, the limitations that Abe's blindness imposed on them. There were so many things that he couldn't do—ordinary, simple things like going to the movies or wandering around the shops. He did ask her whether she would like to go to the movies, but she didn't really see what fun it could be for him, only able to hear the dialogue. Likewise the swimming pools, the ice rink, the tennis courts . . . what good were they to Abe? He couldn't swim or skate in vast throngs of people. This question of "what to do" had never bothered them in Star Street—there had always been a multitude of things to do. The fact that Abe couldn't see had never caused them any problems. It was the stultifying effect of the guesthouse room and the rain that was dulling their inventiveness.

By the following Thursday the rain had stopped and the skies were clear. Abe was all for going straight out, but two weeks of punching a cash register under artificial light (two weeks, also, of running the risk of discovery every time she came to see him) were beginning to take their toll. She felt tired and grumpy, disinclined to do anything save fling herself on to Abe's bed and lie there in a heap. He tried without success to shame her out of it—"It's all very well for you, you can go for a walk whenever you feel like it. I have to rely on other people."

She only scowled and muttered, "You haven't been working."

"Oh! Haven't I? What do you think that is?" He waved a hand toward his typemachine. It still had a piece of paper rolled into it. "Next semester's courses, that's what that is. I suppose you picture me lying flat on my back all day?"

She mumbled ungraciously.

"What was that?" said Abe.

"I said, at least you haven't had to be sitting behind a cash register making asinine conversation about the price of butter."

"Wouldn't mind the chance. Better than being cooped up here."

"That's what you think."

"It's what I *know* . . . you wouldn't want to do a swap."

She found it more convenient to ignore that. "Anyway," she said, changing tack, "*why* are you all cooped up? I thought you were supposed to be apartment hunting with Stephen."

"I am—or rather, I was. I was going to tell you about it, only you've been so full of self-pity. . . . I believe I may actually have found somewhere."

A momentary flicker of optimism caused her to roll over on her side, propped on one elbow. "Where?"

"Just fifteen minutes away—basement apartment in an old house. Two bedrooms, one sitting room, own kitchen, own bath . . . couldn't be better."

"Sounds too good to be true. Where did you find it?"

"Ah. Well—" He made a face. "To be perfectly honest, it's a bit of a cheat. From a friend of a friend who Does Things for the Blind—and did a bit of sentimental string-pulling while she was about it. Seeing as I am judged to be in special and particular need, etc., etc. I don't usually take advantage of that sort of thing, but just for once—"

"You really think they'll let you have it?"

"Well . . . they know the worst about me."

"Hm!" She would believe it when it happened. She collapsed again on to the bed. "Probably discover at the last minute they're anti-Semitic and won't have any Jews in the place . . . bound to be *some*thing wrong. Either you can't see or you've got the wrong shape nose or you play the piano —that'll be the next thing: no pianos on premises. Upset the neighbors. They'll find *some*thing, don't you worry."

There was silence, then Abe said: "The way you put it, I don't seem to have very much going for me, do I?"

"Now who's being self-pitying? Oh, Abe!" Remorsefully, she hurled herself at him, both arms about his neck. "I'm sorry! I'm sorry! I didn't mean it!"

"No; I know you didn't."

"It wasn't anything against *you*—"

"That's okay. You don't have to explain. It's just the situation, getting on top of us. But we mustn't let it, do you see? That's the whole object of the exercise. To demonstrate to your mother that being sixteen doesn't mean being irresponsible—and that being twenty-four doesn't mean being unable to control oneself. Which is why"—he stood up, pulling her with him—"I would rather we didn't take any chances. If we go out, we remove all temptation. If we stay in—"

"What?" she said.

"It makes it very difficult. Do I have to spell it out?"

Defiantly, she said, "What would it matter?"

"It would matter."

"Why?"

"Because it would."

"That's no answer!" She thought of Mary-Jane and Barry. "Some of the girls at school—"

"I am not interested," said Abe, "in some of the girls at school. I'm interested in you and me and in not blotting our copy-book. So come on! Stir yourself! The sun's out, the rain's stopped. Take me somewhere different. I'm tired of the town hall gardens."

On Saturday he told her that Donald was coming down during the week and they were going to have a look at the apartment together; on Thursday he told her that it was "all secured, bar the shouting."

"You mean you've got it?" She was almost beside herself. "Abe, you've *got* it?"

"Subject to references. Shouldn't be any problem there."

"Well, don't sound so *calm* about it! Aren't you thrilled? Aren't you excited?"

"Yes, of course I am."

"Then why don't you sound it? Abe?" She looked up at him, suddenly anxious. "You're not having second thoughts, are you?"

"I don't know, I—" He shook his head. "I can't help wondering if Donald really knows what he's taking on—if *I* really know what I'm taking on."

"Abe, you can't back out *now*!"

"No, I'm not going to back out. I just—"

"It'll be all right—you'll see!" She took his hand in hers. "I'll come over. I'll help."

"You'd better! I'm counting on you. You just make sure you're available the Sunday after next."

"Is that when you move in?"

"Supposed to be."

"Then I'll stay and cook dinner—special house-warming! Oh, Abe, come on! Be brave! It's an adventure, isn't it?"

He grinned. "I guess. Want to come and have a gander? Just from the outside? And if it looks like an ancient monument in the last stages of decay, you don't have to bother telling me. . . ."

When she left him that evening she was happier than she had been for weeks. Abe in his own apartment was not the same as Abe in Star Street, but it was a thousand times better than Abe at the Briarley. Already she could picture the meals they would cook together, the parties there would be. She burst into the house thinking that tonight she could forgive even her mother, cause of all their recent misery though she was. Tea was on the kitchen table—they were back, she noted, to ordinary jam and plain spongecake—but her mother didn't say her usual "Good. Just in time. The kettle's only this minute boiled." Instead, her face grim, she said, "And where exactly have you been?"

Did hearts really miss beats? Did they really stand still? Or was it just that they seemed to do so?

She stammered, "You know where I've been."

"I do not know where you've been. I thought that I knew —because I thought that you had told me. It seems a strange way to rehearse, walking the streets with Abe."

Her cheeks flared up. "He's found an apartment—we went to look at it."

"And last Saturday? In the town hall gardens?"

She opened her mouth to say something; but what was there to say?

"I haven't been spying on you," said Mrs. Fenton. "I never thought that there would be any need. It was Peggy who happened to mention it."

Peggy. She had been right all along to hate that woman. Mrs. Fenton shook her head.

"She wasn't spying either. It may surprise you to know that people actually do have better ways of passing their time. She simply mentioned it as a point of interest—'I saw your daughter with her young man again.' She said she'd seen you last week as well. Holding hands in the town hall gardens."

"So? It's no crime to hold someone's hand, is it?"

"Not at all. Peggy seemed to think it rather touching. I might think it rather touching myself if it weren't for the nasty taste left in my mouth from the lies that you told me."

"I didn't tell you any lies! I told you that I was going to rehearsal—"

"At your friend Hilary's. Up near Lloyd Park."

"I said *usually*—*usually* we went to Hilary's."

"But you haven't been to Hilary's for the past two weeks, because Hilary is away and no rehearsals have been held. I called Stephen's mother."

She was insulted. "You mean you've been *checking up* on me? With a *stranger?*"

"I felt it was about time. *You* obviously had no intention of telling me."

"There isn't anything to tell—we haven't *done* anything! It's only you and your vile imaginings—"

"You've gone behind my back; can you wonder if I have vile imaginings? As a matter of fact, I don't—or at any rate, I didn't. When people tell you lies—yes, lies! Lies by implication—you naturally begin to ask yourself what they have to hide. If you wanted to see Abe, why didn't you come straight out with it?"

"Because I didn't think you'd let me, that's why! Because I know perfectly well why you got rid of him—because you discovered that in spite of being blind he wasn't a eunuch—because you thought he was going to *defile* me—"

"Oh, don't be so melodramatic!"

"Well, didn't you? Didn't you tell *me* lies by implication? All that crud about the piano and the neighbors. Why didn't you tell me the truth? You didn't want us getting too friendly in case he screwed me!"

She knew as soon as she had said it that she had gone too far. Mrs. Fenton never objected to the odd damn and blast, she was even prepared to put up with the occasional bloody hell or Christ, but there were some expressions she drew the line at, and screwed was one of them. Her face hardened. Coldly, she said, "If that is the sort of language which you and Abe habitually employ—"

"Abe doesn't employ it! You know bloody well he doesn't!"

She had already gone one step too far; the rest, now, seemed inevitable. "Don't try putting the blame on him: *he*'s not the one that teaches me bad language. If you want to know where I get it from, then I get it from school—that nice, posh, paid-for school. And *they* don't only *talk* about it—they *do* it. Abe doesn't . . . he's too worried trying to prove to you that even if he is twenty-four he's not going to turn around and rape me. *He*'s never laid a finger on me."

Tight-lipped, Mrs. Fenton said, "If Abe is so worried about trying to prove things to me, it might have been better had he not gone behind my back."

"He didn't go behind your back! He was the one who told me I'd got to get your permission."

"Then it was a great pity that you didn't. Had you come to me and asked me, 'May I go on seeing Abe?'—"

"Why should I have to *ask* you? What's it got to *do* with you? I could be out earning my own living!"

"You could, but you're not, so—"

"So whose fault is that? Who wanted me to stay on?"

"I did, your headmistress did—one of the main reasons being that we both felt you were too immature to know what was best for yourself. Your behavior these past two weeks just shows me how right I was. If you behave like a child, then you'll have to be treated as a child. You can telephone Abe and tell him that thanks entirely to your own stupid, underhanded way of carrying on, the old cow has got her knickers in a twist—I don't doubt that is the way you will put it—and that it might be wiser if you didn't see each other any more. You can also t—"

"I won't!" She screamed it at her mother across the table. "You've got no right—you don't own me! It's my life, I'll run it how I like!"

"Not while you're in this house, you won't. You either do as you're told or you get out."

"Then I'll get out!"

The kitchen door slammed behind her. She snatched her bicycle out of the shed. Not since she was a tiny child had she run away from home. In those days it had been a regular occurrence. "I'll run away if you treat me like that!" Inevitably, the answer had come back: "Go along, then . . . run." It had all been a game in those days; this time it was in earnest. She had got out, and she was staying out. There could be no going back.

19

>>>

SHE RAN TO ABE BECAUSE HE WAS THE ONLY PERSON SHE could run to. Some wild notion she had of seeking sanctuary. She could spend the night with him at the Briarley—Mrs. Busby wouldn't mind, just the one night. Next day they could go somewhere else, where they weren't known—they could buy a ring, say they were married, why shouldn't they? What was to stop them? Other people did it. If she was old enough to leave school, she was old enough to live with him. She wouldn't expect him to keep her, she would find herself a job of some kind, a proper job, not just punching cash registers. Something in an office, or—

"And what about your career? I thought I'd sold you the idea of teachers' training college? You'd throw all that out of the window?"

"I could still do it—later. As a mature student. They'd give me a grant."

"And your exams? What would you propose to do about those?"

"I could go on studying in the evenings. At technical college. People do. They—"

"People might," said Abe, "but you're not going to. You're going to go straight back home—"

"No!" She backed away from him. "That's the one thing I'm not going to do!"

"It's the one thing you most certainly are going to do!"

She took up a stance, defiant, across the room. "*You* can't make me!"

"No, I can't make you—in the sense that I can't physically compel you. I'm the easiest person on earth to play blindman's-bluff with; we both know that."

She colored. "That's not what I meant!"

"So what did you mean? That you don't intend listening to anything that I might have to say?"

"There isn't anything *to* say. You don't understand! I'm out—for good!"

Abe shook his head. "Marianne, there isn't anything good about it. It's only going to convince her all the more that we're not to be trusted. I'm not surprised she was mad at you—I'd be mad at you myself, if it weren't for the fact that I feel I'm largely to blame. I ought to have checked. In that sense it's been me as much as you, so—"

"What has? We haven't *done* anything!"

"No, and we're not going to! And don't start telling me about other people. What other people do is their business. What may be right for them isn't necessarily right for us."

Her top lip quivered ominously. "It could be," she said, "if you really wanted it to be."

"And just what do you mean by that remark?"

"I mean that if you really felt that w-way ab-bout me—"

"Yes? What would I do? Throw you on the bed and rape you?"

"You wouldn't have to r-rape me. I'd be p-perfectly w-willing."

Abe said coldly, "Well, I wouldn't."

"Because you don't feel that way, that's w-why!"

"Of course I *feel that way*—for God's sake! Use a bit of imagination! How do you *think* I feel? I'm only human, aren't I? I may not be able to see, but I still have all my other faculties."

"Then why—"

"Because I'm eight years older than you, that's why!"

"But you'll *always* be eight years older than me—"

"Yes; but you won't always be sixteen. . . . Marianne, come on! Pull yourself together." He held out a hand, but she stood where she was, refusing to take it. "Be a good girl and go home—it's the only sensible thing to do. I know your mother. She won't stay angry for very long, especially if you have the guts to go back now and face the music. All you have to do is say you're sorry. Admit you should have asked her permission. That's all it takes; it's not so very much. Not when you think what's at stake. If you like I'll come with you, but I honestly think it would be better if you did it on your own. I don't mind coming over tomorrow, if you feel it would help; but for tonight—"

All she said in reply was "If you made me pregnant, there's nothing she could do about it."

"On the contrary," retorted Abe, "if I made you pregnant, there is everything she could do about it! That is quite one of the silliest things I have ever heard you say. It makes me ashamed of you—behaving like a child."

She said venomously, "Well, if everybody will insist on treating me like one—"

"So which comes first, the chicken or the egg? Don't be so ridiculous! You just do as I say, and—"

"And *what*? I'm sick of doing as you say! Where's it got us? Nowhere! All you ever do is take her side. You haven't any *back*bone!"

She wrenched open the door. Abe said sharply, "Marianne! Where are you going?" He made a dive toward her, but already she was out on the landing, already hurtling three at a time down the stairs. She heard his voice—"Marianne! Come back!"—but too late; she had gone.

She headed instinctively for the one place that she knew— the one place where she might be alone, to lick her wounds. She left her bike, as usual, chained to the churchyard railings, set off by the side of the cottages, up the path through the woods. Two weeks of heavy rain had reduced the ground to a mire. She slipped and stumbled, now squelching through glutinous bog, now up to her ankles in mud, scarcely caring for the state of her jeans or shoes. The chalk path was churned to a cakey mess, treacherous as a skating rink. Torrential downpours had carried away part of the side of the quarry, so that where once there had been fencing there was now a gaping hole. She kept well away from it, plowing through the sticky gray sludge of the chalk, over the stile into the buttercup field, wet as a water meadow, on across the marshy ground till she came at last to the Kingdom.

In spite of the torrents, it was quite dry in her domain. Only one pool of water, where the roof had leaked, and most of that caught in the plastic bucket she always left in position just in case. The wind had obviously blown from the right direction, driving the rain against the back wall rather than the windows. She took off her sodden shoes and socks, peeled off her jeans, laid them out to dry on the chair that had no back, wrapped herself in the old army blanket, and without any warning fell asleep.

It was really quite extraordinary, because she never fell asleep just like that. She always had to think herself into it. Today she closed her eyes for no more than a second and was gone. When she opened them again, the light had changed from early evening to late. The sun no longer poured in through the windows, the shadows were deepening perceptibly even as she looked, crawling with long fingers across the floor. She saw by her watch that it was almost ten o'clock. At first she refused to believe it—she thought her watch must have galloped—but one glance outside the door showed her that it was so. The countryside wore a definite aspect of approaching night. The birds were silent, all the busy daytime creatures gone to their nests and their burrows. There was an air of stealth as the night patrols took over.

She had never stayed in the Kingdom so late. Her mother would be in a fine panic—or there again, perhaps she wouldn't. Perhaps she had washed her hands of her. Simply shrugged her shoulders and said, Let her get on with it. . . . No. In her heart she knew that her mother never would. In a moment of anger she might tell her to "either do as you're told or get out," but she would never close the door in her face. She would never stop caring. By now she would almost certainly have telephoned Abe at the Briarley. Abe would have told her what had happened. They would be wondering, worrying. The idea half pleased her, half made her feel guilty. On the one hand, she thought, it serves them right; on the other, I shouldn't have run out on Abe like that. It wasn't fair, running out on someone who couldn't run after you. *I'm the easiest person in the world to play blind-man's-bluff with; we both know that.* And she had done it, hadn't she? She had taken the meanest advantage of him that anyone could. Her cheeks throbbed; she put up her hands to cool them. YOU *can't make me*—oh, but she hadn't meant it that way! She hadn't!

For a moment her impulse was to jump up and go running straight back to him, to fling both her arms about his neck and beg his forgiveness. He surely wouldn't hold it against her? He must know that she would never intentionally do anything to hurt him. But then, she thought, if she went back now, what would she have achieved? Nothing. All would be as it was before. Abe would still be eight years older than she was, she would still be "only sixteen," her mother still would not want her to go on seeing him. Going back was no use. She had to do something—something to prove—

What if she stayed away for a whole twenty-four hours? If she spent the entire night up there in the Kingdom? That would give them something to think about. Perhaps then they might be brought to realize at last that she was serious. Tomorrow she might even take the train and go up to town and . . .

Money?

She pulled her bag toward her—the bag Abe had brought her from Italy. She had her yesterday's pay envelope still in there. She had forgotten about it entirely. She was supposed to put it in the bank each week, accumulating for her vacation. Well, that settled it. She scarcely imagined, as things stood, that she would be allowed to go off for two weeks with Abe, even if the rest of the group was going to be there to play chaperone. She might just as well cut loose, burn her boats. She would go up to town and take the cheapest room she could find, somewhere way over in north London, where they had gone for the Mozart recital. It had looked pretty sleazy out there—Clerkenwell, or wherever it was. Rooms couldn't cost that much. Anyway, first thing Monday morning she would get herself a job. Any job, it wouldn't matter what. She would only be doing it for a few days—maybe a week—two at the very most. It wouldn't take the police (or would it be the Salvation Army?) all that long to trace her. It wasn't as if she were going to assume a false name and identity or make any attempt to cover her tracks. She only wanted to demonstrate that she had meant what she said.

She had half a bar of chocolate in her bag. She ate it and lay down again, pulling the army blanket over her head. Her mother would be nearly frantic by the end of a week. Perhaps she would send her a postcard from somewhere anonymous, like Victoria Station, saying that she was all right. They couldn't accuse her, then, of being thoughtless. She pictured the scene as she was finally brought home in a police car— her mother embracing her, weeping over her, trying to scold and not being able to: "You've been a very naughty girl, you know that, don't you? But now that you're back—"

Now that she was back, all would be forgiven. Her mother would say that she had never fully appreciated how much Abe had meant to her. "I honestly thought that it was just a passing phase."

Yes; that was what Miss Pargeter had always said about everything: *She'll grow out of it: it's just a passing phase.*

"I can see now that I was wrong. I don't mind admitting it. You've demonstrated pretty conclusively that you're old enough to take care of yourself and to know what you're doing. Of course, I couldn't actually allow you to get *married* until after you've left school . . ."

Fitfully, she dozed. She kept dreaming and waking up. The dream was always the same: she and Abe were standing in the center of a great prairie, and they were arguing. She didn't know what they were arguing about, but it always ended the same way, with her running out on him, running, running, across the prairie, until at last she came to a great rift in the rocks, across which she must jump, and every time she jumped she thought, If Abe tries to come after me he will fall over the edge and be killed. . . .

Twice she woke up cold and sweating; twice she fell asleep again. Then came the third time, and the dream turned to nightmare, for now Abe was chasing after her, he was calling to her, he was approaching the rift in the rocks and there was nothing she could do about it, because she was powerless to move or to shout or in any way to warn him.

She woke with a start, and the nightmare continued. His voice was still calling to her, faint and far-off: "Marianne? Marianne?"

He was out there. Somewhere he was out there.

"The quarry," she thought. "*Abe*, the *quarry!*"

She threw off the blanket, hauled on her jeans, thrust bare feet into her shoes, and tore outside, into the darkness.

"Abe!" she called. "*Abe! Keep still and don't move!*"

It was quite impossible he could have heard her. He would have heard her voice, as she had heard his, but not the words. She would have done better not to have called at all. Now he would know for certain that she was there, and it would give him confidence. He would start feeling his way around the edge of the quarry, using the fence as his guide, until he came to the part where there wasn't any, where the chalk was like a skating rink and if he should slip there was nothing to keep him from falling . . .

Heedless of hazards, she set off at a run across the buttercup field. Splashing, slipping, sliding, the breath rasping in her throat, she reached the stile.

"Abe!" she called again. "*Abe!*"

His voice came back: "I'm down here!"

"Then stay put and don't move! Abe! *Don't move!* The fence has gone from the—"

She was too late, by just seconds. He must have taken a step forward even as she called to him.

By the time she reached the spot, he was only a dark shape, huddled at the foot of the quarry.

20

>>>

SHE STILL HAD TO GO INTO THE SUPERMARKET NEXT DAY; TO
sit on her high stool, under the artificial lighting, totting up
the groceries, just the same as usual. She had begged and
pleaded to be let off—"Just the one day! Can't you tell them
I'm not well?"—but Mrs. Fenton wouldn't hear of it. She
said, "Let it be a lesson to you. If you've only had four hours'
sleep, that's your fault. How many do you think I've had? Get
your clothes on and stop wallowing."

Forty minutes later she was punching zombielike at the
cash register, mechanically dishing out plastic bags and
weighing fruit and vegetables. Her mind had never been so
little on her work. How could she concentrate on cans of
salmon and special offers when Abe was lying there in the
hospital? She kept seeing him, huddled at the foot of the
quarry—kept seeing him in the ambulance, not moving, not
speaking, and the ambulance man with his silly jokes, trying
to cheer her up, when what she desperately needed was reas-
surance that Abe was not going to die. And then they had
reached the hospital, and her mother had been there, and
Marianne had done something she had not done since junior
high school: she had burst into tears, and Mrs. Fenton had
put her arms around her and held her, which was something

she had not done since even before Marianne was at junior high school, and they had sat there together, on the hard hospital bench, waiting for news of Abe.

Her mother hadn't made silly jokes to try and cheer her up. When a white-sheeted figure had been wheeled past on a gurney, she hadn't needed to be told what Marianne was thinking. Bracingly she had said, "Don't be so silly, they'd let us know. In any case, Abe's young and fit. He's tough. He'll pull through." She might have added that if he did not the fault would be entirely Marianne's, but she hadn't; not once.

It had been almost half an hour before they had heard that Abe was going to be all right—that as far as could be ascertained he had suffered nothing more serious than a few bruised ribs and a sprained ankle.

"We'll keep him in for the next twenty-four hours, of course, just to be on the safe side, but I don't think the X-rays will show anything. It's really just a precaution."

Her mother had said, "There! What did I tell you?" and given her a hug.

The doctor, with a wink, had said: "So long as you don't try doing that to *him* for the next day or two, young lady. He's going to be just the tiniest bit sore, to say the least."

No one had suggested that Marianne might like to go in and see him before they left. She hadn't liked to suggest it herself. At the back of her mind was the nagging thought: suppose he doesn't want me to? *You haven't any backbone. . . .* How could she have said such a thing? To Abe, of all people? And then to turn and run . . .

Her cheeks roared, hot as blast furnaces. She shook her head, so that her hair fell over them. Running out had been a mean trick to play. Mean and cheap and rotten. Worse even than going off to Switzerland. If there was one thing she knew she ought never, never to do, it was to take advantage of the fact that Abe wasn't the same as other people. That was the one part of the whole affair that was really inexcusable. It was the reason why he probably wouldn't ever want to see her again—and yet she knew that she had to see him. She was the biggest coward on earth, but even she knew that it was up to her.

On her way home after work she went into a flower shop and asked which flowers had the best scent. The woman looked doubtful and said, "Well . . . roses, I suppose, but carnations are cheaper."

"Then I'll have roses," said Marianne.

She bought half a dozen red ones, even though they were the most expensive, plus some green frondy stuff to go with them. The frondy stuff didn't have any scent, but at least he would be able to feel it and know that she hadn't cheated him—that there hadn't been any question of "Oh, it's only Abe. *He* can't tell."

Mrs. Fenton was in the kitchen, washing up the morning's breakfast dishes. She said, "I hope you remembered the chops, or it'll have to be baked beans again." And then, turning around from the sink: "Roses! Good heavens! I suppose they're not meant for Abe, by any chance?"

"Yes." She clutched them to her chest, instantly on the defensive. "Why shouldn't they be? There's nothing wrong with giving flowers to a man, is there? Just because he's a man? You like flowers when you're in the hospital. Why shouldn't—"

"All right, all right! There's no need to get uptight! I'm not suggesting you shouldn't give him flowers, I'm just trying to tell you that he's no longer there. His sister called a few minutes ago. She's taking him back to London with her. Are these the chops? I'll get them under way. How do you want them? In the frying pan or under the broiler?"

The question washed over her. She stood, clutching her roses. Absurd red roses at fifty pence a throw. Green frondy stuff to go with them. And Abe no longer here. Abe back in London.

"To*night*?" she said. "He's going to*night*?"

"Apparently. It seemed there wasn't any reason for his staying on; the X-rays didn't show anything. Just bruising, luckily. She was very nice about it. Do you want rice or potatoes? Let's have rice. It's easier. She wanted to know whether you would like to go up there for tea on Sunday. She said if you could manage to get to Victoria about four o'clock, she'd meet you in the car. Well?" She thrust a saucepan at Marianne. "Did you hear what I said? You've got an invitation to tea. That ought to please you."

Yes, she thought. But it wasn't Abe who had asked her, was it? She took the saucepan, tossed the roses onto the table.

"You might as well have them now," she said. "I can't take him roses when he's not in the hospital. In any case"—she stumped across to the sink—"I guess I owe it to you."

It wasn't Abe who had asked her, so what did it matter what she wore? *He* couldn't see, and probably wouldn't care even if he could. On the other hand, there was still Sarah to consider. She ought to make at least some sort of an attempt at sophistication. Her mother, trying to be helpful, said, "Why don't you wear that nice little blue dress with the puff sleeves?" She rejected the little blue dress contemptuously.

She had gone beyond the stage of little blue dresses, with or without puff sleeves.

On Saturday, during her lunch break, she took the bus to the center of town and went to the market, where sometimes there were goods that were mysteriously said to have fallen off the backs of trucks and as a result were sold cheap. On a stall next to Fresh Eggs & Dairy Produce she found a flaming scarlet blouse in a slinky sort of satin material, and a black crêpe skirt with a slit down the side. The boy who was selling them didn't actually say they had fallen off the back of anything, but she knew from the price that they must have. Her mother would say they had been stolen. Still, her mother didn't have to know everything.

In Help the Aged she found a pair of sandals with heels so tall they almost walked on tiptoe. She tried them on and they were exactly her size, though she did rather wonder if she dared. In the end, because they were only fifty pence—"need soling and heeling, dear," but what did it matter, just for the one day?—she suppressed her inner qualms and took possession of them. A rope of big brassy beads from Freedom from Hunger completed the outfit, successfully, she thought. She tried everything on in front of the mirror before going to bed, and no one would have known that she was still at school. Sarah Lawrence needn't think she always went round with her hair looking like rats' tails and her feet in Hush Puppies. She could be as sophisticated as anyone when she put her mind to it.

Not until the next day, when it actually came to getting dressed, did the doubts begin to creep in. Was the blouse just a tiny bit—not gaudy, but . . . tartish? Could she really manage to totter on six-inch heels without falling flat on her face? Suppose she got one caught in a grating and ripped it right off?

Well, she wouldn't have to get one caught in a grating, would she? She would just have to look where she was going. And the blouse wasn't tartish, it was simply that she was too accustomed to the boring bottle greens and navy blues that Mrs. Fenton insisted on because of their not showing the dirt.

She slung Abe's leather bag over her shoulder and walked downstairs as nonchalantly as a person can who is having to concentrate on not breaking her neck. Her mother was in the front room. She supposed she would have to announce the fact of her departure. She did her best to put only her head around the door and keep the rest of herself hidden, but Mrs. Fenton, seemingly immersed in the Sunday paper, snatched off her glasses and shrieked, "You're never going out dressed like that?"

Marianne stiffened. "What's wrong with this?"

"You want people to take you for a streetwalker? For goodness' sake! Go back upstairs and put something else on."

This time last week she would have said, "For crying out *loud!*" and in all probability slammed the door behind her. She would have clumped back up to her bedroom in a fury, and as a mark of defiance arrayed herself in the baggiest sweater and the shabbiest jeans that she could find. Today she said, "Oh, if I *must*," and five minutes later reappeared, defiant, in the little blue dress with the puff sleeves.

"That's better," said Mrs. Fenton. "You look quite pretty."

"Makes me feel about fourteen."

"Yes, well, never mind how it makes *you* feel. Try thinking of Abe for a change. He doesn't want you turning up looking like something out of the back streets of Soho."

She would have been happier if she could have felt that he wanted her to turn up at all. Long before her train drew into Victoria, she had managed to convince herself that he did

not. She could picture all too clearly how it must have been.
His sister, well meaning, would have sprung it on him as a
surprise. She could hear the dialogue, running through her
head:

ABE'S SISTER (in motherly tones, brightly): By the way, I
    asked your little girl friend to come for tea.
ABE (in undisguised horror): You did *what*?
ABE'S SISTER Asked her to come to tea. I thought you'd be
    pleased.
ABE   Well, I'm not. I don't want to see her.
ABE'S SISTER (aggrieved): So how was I to know? Well, it's
    too late to put her off now. You'll just have to
    make the best of it . . .

She didn't pray for the train to crash. There wasn't any
point. She had proved in the past that prayers were no use.
All you could do was grit your teeth and go through with
things.

She saw Abe's sister almost at once. She was standing by
the W. H. Smith bookstall, in the center of the main con-
course. She would have known it was his sister even if she
hadn't brought Sarah with her to prove the fact. It was Sarah
(all got up like a dog's dinner in cream silk) who spotted
Marianne. She said something to her mother, and her mother
turned and smiled and held out a hand and said, "Hallo,
Marianne! How nice to meet you at long last. I've heard so
much about you." Who from? she wondered. From Abe? Or
from Sarah?

Sarah said, "Abe's in the car—because of his ankle. It's
lucky it wasn't his wrist. It could have been fatal."

"Rubbish!" Her mother gave her a little push. "Don't be so

melodramatic. It's a slight sprain, Marianne. That's all. Nothing in the least to get worked up about."

"It could have been," said Sarah.

"Well, it could have been, but it wasn't. You don't have to worry." She gave Marianne's arm a friendly squeeze. "He's pretty indestructible. We discovered that when he was a little boy . . . I don't think anyone ever fell out of more trees or into more rivers or off more garden sheds than that one. Here we are." She had come to a halt beside a long, sleek, powder-blue car. "Would you like to climb in the back with Sarah?"

She would rather not have, but obviously she had to. Abe was sitting in the front, in the passenger seat. As she slid in, onto the softness of the leather, he turned and said, "Hallo, you! Come to gloat?" She didn't know what to say. She didn't know whether he was joking or whether he really meant it. She wanted most desperately to tell him that she was sorry— but how could she, with other people there? She sat tongue-tied, cheeks growing slowly scarlet.

It was Abe's sister who came to the rescue. Briskly she said, "Cut the self-pity. Why isn't your seat belt fastened?"

"Because I unfastened it."

"What for?"

"Because I was going to get out."

"Well, do it up again. I'm not taking the responsibility for you going through the windshield. If you make all this fuss over one sprained ankle, God only knows what you'd do with a lacerated forehead."

Once Marianne might have giggled to hear Abe being treated like a child by his elder sister. Now she didn't like to, in case it should offend.

The Lawrences lived in Chelsea, in a block of what were, quite unmistakably, luxury apartments. There was carpet in the entrance hall, even carpet in the elevator. Everything was very silent and hermetic. Abe's sister said, "Sarah, show Marianne where she can tidy up," and she found herself promptly borne off down a long, white, noiseless corridor into far-off regions entirely remote from the rest of the apartment. Sarah, self-important, the pleats of her cream silk skirt swinging to and fro as she walked, played graciously at hostess.

"I'm afraid Daddy isn't here just at the moment—he has to go away quite a lot. He's in oil, you see. One has to travel. Grandma's not here either. She would have been, if we'd told her—about Abe, I mean. Mummy wanted to, but he made her promise not to. He said he didn't want her upset. I suppose she is getting on a bit, and Cheshire is quite a long way. This one's my room." She threw open a door. "That one over there"—she pointed—"is Abe's. Would you like to see it? I can show you if you want. Abe won't mind. I go in and out all the time." She paused, glancing slyly up at Marianne from beneath thick black lashes. "Mummy says I shouldn't. How Victorian can you get?"

"I wouldn't call it Victorian," said Marianne. "She probably just thinks you're making a nuisance of yourself."

Sarah tossed her head. "Well, I'm not. Abe doesn't think so. Anyway, it isn't *that* that bothers her. You'd better wash your hands, we shall be having tea in a moment."

They went back down the long white corridor into the most enormous room that Marianne had ever seen, with ceilings almost out of sight and windows that went down to the floor. Abe was already there, sprawled at his ease on a red velvet sofa. He looked up as they came in and said, "Been shown round the ancestral barracks?" in perfectly equable tones, not at all as if he resented her being there, but he didn't pat the sofa or do anything to indicate that she might like to sit next to him. It was Sarah who sat next to Abe; Marianne was banished to an armchair (likewise red velvet) about half a mile away. She wondered what exactly was happening. She had thought they were supposed to be having tea, but she couldn't see any table laid. Perhaps they were waiting for a call to troop out to the kitchen for sardines on toast or paste sandwiches.

She was appalled when the double doors opened and Abe's sister came in with a cart and she realized that they were expected to eat where they were. (Eat *here*? Over the rose-pink carpet, sitting on the red velvet chairs?) She glanced at Abe and Sarah, but neither of them appeared to find anything odd in the proceedings. It seemed that "tea," in Chelsea, was not the hearty sitting-up-at-table-with-bread-and-jam-and-homemade-cakes variety such as she was accustomed to, but a social juggling act with plates balanced on knees and tea-cups perched on little tables and nothing but a stiff white napkin spread between you and disaster. The tea itself came faintly scented, without any milk, and was sipped from thimble-sized cups that were almost transparent, and fragile as eggshells, so that with huge gangling hands like hers you scarcely dared take proper hold for fear of breakage. As for the food—the wafer-thin slivers of bread and butter and the tiny, dolls' house sandwiches; the shiny white meringues and the bowls full of real strawberries and cream—that was wheeled to and fro on the silent silver cart across the rose-pink acres by Sarah, very prim and proper. "More *tea*, Marianne? More bread and *butter*, Marianne?" It was all rather like being in the Ritz (how she imagined it would be, being in the Ritz). Deep down inside herself she knew that her mother had been quite right about the little blue dress—she also knew that it was going to be only a question of time before she disgraced herself by spilling tea or dripping globs of cream. An accident of some kind was inevitable.

Since it was inevitable, it could actually have been worse: only bread and butter on the carpet, and even then it landed right-side up, so there wasn't the least need for Sarah to go springing to her feet in pursuit of sponges and mops. Her mother was evidently of the same mind. Quite sharply, she said, "Sit down, Sarah. Don't fuss."

"But it'll tread in," said Sarah.

"It will not tread in. There is nothing to tread. Get on with your tea."

Abe said, "Is that Marianne being clumsy? What is it this time? *Not* the bone china! She's worse than I am, and *she* hasn't even got an excuse."

"You just shut up," said his sister. "You'd better not talk —I still remember that dreadful children's party at the Rosenbergs' where you not only sent a bucket of ice water all over the little Glazer girl, who screamed her head off, but then had the appalling greed to snaffle *two* cream pyramids when you were only supposed to have one. Never shall I forget the shame of it! *Where's the last cream pyramid? Why hasn't Johnny got a cream pyramid?* And then the Glazer girl piping up . . . *Please, Mrs. Rosenberg, Abraham Shonfeld's eaten two!*"

Marianne giggled in spite of herself. Sarah shot her an angry glance of reproach.

"He couldn't help it," she said.

There was a silence. Marianne stopped giggling. Abe said, "*Oy vay!*" and closed his eyes. Quite suddenly the atmosphere was full of tensions. She couldn't decide whether it was her fault for giggling, or whether it was because of something else.

Then Sarah's mother, looking across at Sarah, said, "How silly of me! I forgot to bring in the chocolate cake. Would you mind going and fetching it?" Sarah, with a slight pout, left the room.

Abe opened his eyes. He said, "Really, I sometimes wonder if I oughtn't to be put in a home."

"Yes—for oversensitive neurotics! Look, I know it's getting on your nerves, but it's just a phase she's going through. You don't have to overplay it."

"*I* can't help it—she said so, didn't she? You heard her: *he couldn't help it* . . . I'm beginning to feel like a two-year-old trapped in the body of a man."

"Oh, don't be so ridiculous. Honestly!" Abe's sister turned, mock-despairing to Marianne. "Is he like this with you?"

Marianne shook her head shyly.

"Well, of course I'm not," said Abe. "Marianne doesn't treat me like a half-wit; *She* just leads me to dance around the edges of open quarries. At least when I fall in she doesn't say, 'Oh, he can't help it.' "

His sister set down her plate. "I think after tea," she said, "we'll have some music."

At eight o'clock they took Marianne back to Victoria Station. This time Sarah sat in the front of the car and Abe sat with Marianne in the back. When they reached the station and she had said her thank-you-very-much-for-having-me's, Abe said, "I'll come and see you to the train."

Sarah instantly bounced around in her seat. "You oughtn't to walk on that ankle, the doctor said so."

"And who did he say it to?" said Abe. "He said it to me."

"But it'll all swell up."

"So it'll all swell up! So whose ankle is it? Yours or mine?"

For just a second she was disconcerted; then brightly, undoing her seat belt, she said, "I'd better come with you, then. You'll need someone to bring you back."

"Sarah!" Her mother's voice held a note of warning. "Let Abe find his own way. He's perfectly capable of it."

"Yes, I know. I just thought—"

"Well, don't. You and I will wait here."

Abe and Marianne walked slowly through the station. Marianne felt almost as awkward, as ill at ease, as she had all those months ago, taking him to the bus stop on the very first day.

"What are you wearing?" said Abe. "Are you wearing a dress?"

"Old blue thing." She muttered it disparagingly. "*She* made me."

"Really? Well, that's nice. Makes a change from jeans." He slipped his arm companionably through hers. "Not still cross with me, are you?"

"*Me?*" She swallowed. "C-cross with *you?*"

"Like you were on Thursday . . . all because I wouldn't rape you!"

Now he was teasing her. She scowled, scuffing her feet through a pile of weekend debris.

" 'Course not. Don't be silly."

"So who's being silly? *I* wasn't the one to go running off in a huff . . . daft bitch! Did you know that I went to see your mother?"

"Yes, she—she told me."

The next morning, over breakfast, she had said that Abe

had been over. She had said, "What he sees in you is quite beyond me to imagine. Only let the least little thing happen to upset you, and you behave like a thwarted child. I have to assume the fault lies in your upbringing, which doesn't reflect very well upon *me*. I can only give us both the benefit of the doubt and assume that if he thinks you're worth nearly breaking his neck over, then there must be some good in you somewhere. Let us just hope that he manages to unearth it."

"Your mother," said Abe, "is okay."

"Yes," she said. She said it very somberly. "I know."

"I always told you that she was, but you would never believe me."

"I did really. It was just—" She broke off, kicking at an empty beer can. "Abe," she said, "I—I never meant you to come after me."

"You mean," said Abe, "you never thought that I could—you never thought that I would have the guts. After all, I'm not supposed to have any backbone, am I?"

"I didn't mean it! You know I didn't mean it!"

"All right, don't go and ruin everything by apologizing. *I* don't mind you telling me I haven't any backbone."

"But I didn't *mean* it. I—"

"Marianne!" He stopped, forcing her to stop with him. "I said *don't*." He gave her a little shake. "Right? Right! What time is your train?"

She craned back, over her shoulder, toward the indicator board. "There's one in about . . . five minutes."

"Where from?"

"Platform twelve."

"Are we near platform twelve?"

"Yes."

"Good. So let's stand still a minute. You haven't forgotten about next weekend, I trust?"

"N-next w-weekend?" Her heart gave a great bound.

"I'm relying on you," said Abe. "You'd better not let me down. . . . I was hoping Thursday evening we might be able to start shifting some of my junk. Make less work for Sunday."

"You mean—you're still moving? Into the apartment?"

"You're dead right I am! My God! You really *do* think I haven't any backbone, don't you?"

"No! But—"

"Now what's the matter?"

She said, "Sarah's coming."

She was trotting determinedly toward them like a little thoroughbred pony. Abe said, "For crying out loud! Does she think I can't even walk a hundred yards by myself?"

"Don't be mad at her," said Marianne. She could afford to be magnanimous—she who knew so well the dread pangs of jealousy, the terrible desire to possess. "You're only going to be here another week. In any case . . . she's only trying to be helpful."

"Oh, sure," said Abe, "sure. Even blow my nose for me, given half the chance. Well?" He turned as he heard her approach. "Did you think I'd eloped, or something?"

Sarah flushed. "We had to move the car. We were blocking the taxi stand."

"I see," said Abe. He said it in the tones of controlled exasperation used by Miss Jones when someone was explaining for the third week in succession why she hadn't been able to get through her homework.

"I thought you mightn't know where we were."

"No. Well, I don't suppose I would have, would I? And that

034

would have been catastrophic, wouldn't it? I might even have had to stand and wait for you to come and find me, mightn't I?"

Sarah's blush deepened and became painful.

"It's all right," said Marianne. Never had she thought the day would come when she would feel sorry for Sarah. "I've got to go, anyway. If I don't dash, they'll close the barriers." She touched Abe lightly on the arm. "See you Thursday," she said.

About the Author

>>>

Jean Ure has written four novels for young adults, all of which were published in England, and makes her American debut with *See You Thursday*. She lives in London.